## She willi... what he asked for

"Is this comfort you're offering," Blade asked, his mouth coming to rest on the soft hollow at the base of her throat, "or something else, Eden?"

The words didn't impinge. Until his hand slid up and cupped her breast.

The gentle touch branded her right through her skin to her bones, setting every cell and nerve end on fire. Automatically she pulled away, her soft red mouth trembling with shock, her eyes dilated and dazedly green in her flushed face.

He wasn't smiling, as she had half thought he might be. With an impassive face, he surveyed her with insulting detachment, obviously not nearly as affected as she had been by those wild kisses.

Then, because she could still feel his touch and because it didn't seem as though he was going to say anything, she whispered, "I don't think that was a good idea."

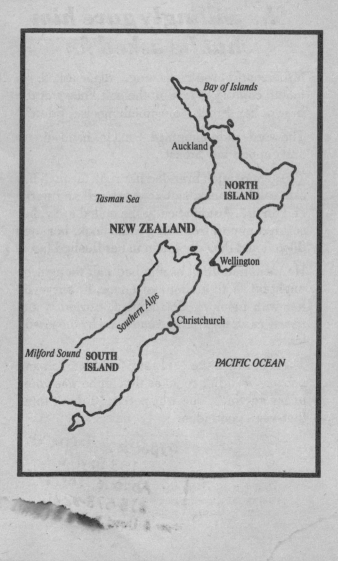

Bay of Islands

Auckland

**NORTH ISLAND**

*Tasman Sea*

**NEW ZEALAND**

Wellington

*Southern Alps*

Christchurch

Milford Sound **SOUTH ISLAND**

*PACIFIC OCEAN*

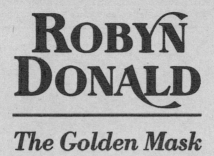

# ROBYN DONALD

## The Golden Mask

**Harlequin Books**

TORONTO • NEW YORK • LONDON
AMSTERDAM • PARIS • SYDNEY • HAMBURG
STOCKHOLM • ATHENS • TOKYO • MILAN
MADRID • WARSAW • BUDAPEST • AUCKLAND

Harlequin Presents first edition March 1993
ISBN 0-373-11537-7

Original hardcover edition published in 1992
by Mills & Boon Limited

THE GOLDEN MASK

# CHAPTER ONE

EDEN ROGERS pushed a thin, tanned hand through the sticky strands of her hair. Beneath her the gelding ambled gently across crisp grass, but, in spite of the fact that she was dying for the cup of tea she was going to make as soon as she got down to the homestead, Eden was so tired that it didn't occur to her to encourage Rusty to move faster.

Her bones ached, her arms and back and legs were going to be stiff tomorrow, she was sunburnt, but at least the calves were now drenched against worms. Scanning the cattle she was driving ahead of her, she smiled at the small black calves frolicking beside their mothers. It was all worth it—even, she thought distastefully, the coat of dust and sweat that stuck unpleasantly to her fine skin.

Thin dark brows drawn together, she gazed around. It was spring, and although the grass made a thick sward there was a tell-tale yellowness to it that spoke of too many years without enough fertiliser. Not that it was any use worrying. This year there was no money for any fertiliser at all.

Normally Eden slept each night as though someone had hit her on the head, but occasionally a lethal combination of exhaustion and apprehension forced a few tears from her. In the morning she managed to disguise the marks on her tanned, fine-boned face, for the one constant concern in her life was that she not worry her grandfather. Sam Rogers was eighty, tired and sick, waiting for death. He was all she had.

He hated being left alone while she went out each day, but it had to be done; there was no one else to work Onemahutu. At least he could now get around the house with the aid of sticks, although he spent most of the lonely days dozing in his chair.

The cattle spread out across the sward were Onemahutu's future, the lifeline. There were too few of them to carry such a baggage of hopes and dreams.

'OK, Jade,' Eden called, leaning over to close the gate. Sagging, it caught on the dry ground, and, swearing in a manner that would have shocked her mother and grandparents, she dismounted to lead Rusty through before dragging the lichened wooden thing back into place.

Yet another job to be done—when she could find the money to buy a gate. This one was past mending. For a moment she stood, face pressed into the warm, sweat-streaked flank of the horse, but Rusty stamped a hoof, wanting to get back to his horse paddock, and Jade the dog whined uneasily.

'All right,' Eden said in a cracked voice, swinging stiffly into the saddle again. She was so tired!

Since the stroke that had weakened her grandfather two years ago she had had to be the strong one, watching with anguish as he slowly lost the will to live and sank further and further into a sad parody of the upright man he had been for seventeen of her nineteen years.

She wiped the dust and the sweat from her forehead with her cloth hat, squinting against the bright sun. Only early November, there was still another month to go before summer was officially here, but the coat of dust caking her features revealed how fast the ground had dried out. Pray God there wasn't going to be a drought. If that happened there was no way they would be able to hold on to Onemahutu.

And if they had to walk off the station her grand-father's dreams would be shattered. That was why Eden worked so hard, struggling with work that was too much for a strong man, let alone a skinny, nineteen-year-old woman.

A light touch on the reins turned the gelding's head towards the highest point of land on the property—a smooth knoll which had a grassy summit shaded by a huge totara tree. Beneath the thick olive canopy was a fenced enclosure, and there rested Eden's mother, who had died of cancer four years ago, and her grandmother, who had followed her within a few months.

Eden often came up here, though seldom of late, since the lambs and calves kept her on the run. Now she dismounted and collapsed on to the grass, resting her head on her arms across her knees for a moment before lifting it to stare with aching green-brown eyes over the acres her grandfather had tended so lovingly, the huge spread of New Zealand countryside that was Onemahutu.

Below, she saw the dull corrugated-iron roof of the homestead, a huge, sprawling, Victorian weatherboard house surrounded by verandas and the overgrown tangle of what had been one of the finest gardens north of Auckland. The swimming pool was a murky green rectangle, the tennis court a paddock that was surrounded by rusty netting hidden beneath a mass of pink-flowered passion-fruit creeper.

Once Onemahutu homestead had been the centre of the district's social life, a place known around New Zealand for its hospitality. Eden could remember the days when no week had gone by without guests—the rich, the famous, the well-connected, and the just plain fascinating ones. They had loved Onemahutu and their gracious, charming hosts. Many still did, but Onemahutu could not afford to entertain now.

Tears of exhaustion squeezed from beneath her dark lashes, streaking the dust on her cheeks. Angrily she wiped them away, her eyes fixed blindly on the thin white stretch of road as it wound its way across the landscape to the homestead. Fumbling, she dragged a handkerchief out and blew her nose. There was still work to be done, and a meal to cook before she would be able to get to bed.

Crying didn't help. It only gave her a headache.

Dust rose in a billowing white cloud, indicating a vehicle on the road. Eden watched it, wondering which of
the families in the three workers' cottages was going to
get a visitor. They were vital to the economy of the
station, those cottages; if it weren't for the rent they
brought in, Onemahutu would have gone under at least
a year ago, if not earlier.

But the vehicle made its slow way past the cottages
and up to the homestead. Perhaps it was Mrs Clare, the
district nurse who came every day to help Sam. But she
normally came in the morning.

'Damn!' Painfully, Eden got to her feet, whistling up
the horse. Rusty had been trained to come to that call,
and, ever eager to get back to his comfortable horse
paddock, he ambled across the grass without demur.

'Home, Rusty. Come on, Jade,' Eden said in the
husky, slightly hesitant voice that, combined with her
reserved manner, made most people think she was shy.

Perhaps if she'd gone away to school she might have
lost that distant air, but she had been educated at home
by correspondence school. She hadn't minded—just as
she didn't mind that the station took all her time and
her exertions, that plotting how to keep it staggering
along occupied her thoughts almost solely. She loved
Onemahutu with a fierce, consuming passion that made
all the hard work, the long hours of back-breaking effort,
worthwhile.

And even if she hadn't loved the wide stretch of hills
and valleys halfway between Northland's east and west
coasts, she would have tried, for more than Onemahutu
Eden loved her grandfather. Two years ago, after he had
been struck down by a stroke, she had faced unflinch-
ingly the fact that if they had to walk off the station he
would have nothing left to live for.

Their accountant had pressed her to put Onemahutu
on the market; he still did, every time he saw her. Then,
as now, she had refused. All they needed, she thought,

swinging into the saddle, was one good season. Well, two good seasons...

Clicking her tongue, she urged the gelding down the hill. Her grandfather found coping with anything other than his normal routine exhausting in the extreme. With any luck the visitor would be one of his old cronies, who for the duration of his visit would take Sam Rogers' mind off his almost complete helplessness.

Eden rode like a stockman: easy in the saddle, wasting neither effort nor energy, her slender figure relaxed yet alert as she put up a hand to drag back a strand of long, darkly ashen hair that was whipping around her face. Normally she wore it yanked up in a pony-tail, but during the afternoon the string had come loose. Her eyes narrowed beneath the brim of her hat as she blew a damp strand from her lips, guiding the gelding down the hill towards the homestead with expert hands.

The car on the overgrown drive was big and solid, white dust coating gleaming maroon paint. It didn't look new, but it was in excellent trim. The visitor was certainly not Mrs Clare. No one Eden knew had a car like that.

Pressing her lips together, she hastily unsaddled and unbridled the horse, rubbed a minute around his ears, and hung the gear up in the shed, then set off for the house.

Eden cast a tired green-brown glance at the overgrown garden. On impulse she wrenched off a rose, brilliantly scarlet, its perfume sweet as paradise. As she discarded her boots and washed her hands and face, the rigid expression that made her look much older softened; she threaded the rose through a buttonhole, hoping that the visitor wouldn't notice that she was still in her working clothes, and that her hair was stringy with the horrible combination of sweat and dust.

Her grandfather's clipped, aristocratic tones floated through the door as she came along the wide passage.

He sounded pleased, with a note in the words that could almost have been excitement.

Summoning a smile, she went in through the door.

And looked straight into the eyes of a man she had never thought to see again.

Blond, with hair the colour of clear honey, he was tall, several inches over six feet, and big-built, with a kind of leashed, self-contained strength that compelled respect and interest. The eyes that captured hers were blue, pale yet vivid, emphasised by dark lashes and brows. There was no emotion discernible in their brilliant depths.

He looked tough yet controlled, a man who knew exactly where he was going, and got there by the shortest route. The boldly arrogant features were carved by a determination Eden recognised with a strange excitement, a sizzling in her bloodstream that threw her completely off balance. At some stage of his career his nose had been broken; it should have coarsened his features, but somehow it only added to that aura of confident authority.

'Ah, Eden.' Her grandfather's voice was a welcome interruption to the bemused whirl of her thoughts. 'You remember Blade Hammond, I'm sure?'

The smile she managed to conjure up wavered as she held out her hand and said like a polite child, 'Yes, of course I do. How are you, Mr Hammond?'

'Blade,' he said, his hard, calloused hand enveloping hers.

If she hadn't felt it, Eden would have scoffed at the notion of electricity zinging from him to her and arcing back again; but she did feel it, so unexpected and intense that it shocked her. Disorientated, she pulled free as quickly as she could. He smiled, and deep in those blazing eyes she thought she saw amusement.

'How about getting us a cup of tea?' Sam suggested in the tone of voice which indicated that this was business.

'Yes, of course,' she said colourlessly.

It hurt when she was relegated to the kitchen. She had worked as hard on Onemahutu as any man, but it had not been enough. To her grandfather she was a woman and therefore her sphere of interest was in the home. Her back-breaking efforts, the fact that he could not give her the leisured social life of parties and balls and young men he thought was her right, all of these conspired to drive him with inner demons. So she conspired with him, pretending that all she had to do was keep the house tidy and act as a gracious hostess.

She made the tea, using the few last pieces of the china her grandmother had brought from England. Even when he had come to Onemahutu five years ago, as boss of the shearing gang, Blade Hammond had not been the sort of man you gave the second-best china to. Eden's hand shook as she poured milk into the jug. This was all that was left of the magnificent china she remembered; two years ago she had sold the dinner sets and the silver, the *objets d'art*, the paintings, even much of the furniture. Incomplete, the tea-set had been worthless, so she'd kept that.

The money had helped buy them time, but that time was fast running out.

So many things had changed, but not Blade. Five years ago he had been every bit as—— She groped for a word, and came up with 'uncompromising'. He'd have been about twenty-two, twenty-three then, yet there had been nothing immature about the autocratic features, or the way he held himself. Now he was almost overpowering, the added maturity intensifying a very masculine arrogance. He was, she thought slowly, every inch her grandfather's equal, and she knew of no man more autocratic than Sam Rogers before he had been struck down.

Why was Blade Hammond here? Had he heard of her grandfather's illness and come on an impulse of kindness? Or had he come for some other reason? Five years ago everyone in the shearing gang had assumed the reason he neither drank nor gambled, nor spent his huge wages on consumer items, was because he intended some day to buy a property. Was that why he had returned? Was he circling Onemahutu like a hawk, marking his prey's weakness?

Eden had longed for someone to take the crushing load of responsibility off her shoulders. Now, faced with the possibility that somehow Blade Hammond had acquired enough capital to think of buying it, she realised that she too would be heartbroken if she had to leave Onemahutu.

Oh, don't be such an idiot! she scoffed, putting out a plate of the biscuits she had baked early that morning. He had probably come to see her grandfather. Bossing a shearing gang earned good money, but good money was not enough to buy a property, not even one in Onemahutu's parlous state.

No doubt he had heard of her grandfather's illness and had come to see him. Which was kind of him. But he had always been kind, even to the fourteen-year-old girl who had conceived a violent crush on him five years ago. Trust her to walk in covered in dust and smelling of cattle and horse! As soon as she had poured the tea she would shower and change.

Carefully she transferred sugar to the bowl, an ironic little smile not softening her wide, soft mouth. The crush of five years ago had been monumental, the sort of passionate falling in love with love that afflicted you when you were fourteen; but she had got over it, and even convinced herself that his image had faded into nothingness. She hadn't thought of him for years.

It was a little upsetting to realise that she had forgotten nothing, not even the tiny fan of lines at the outer edges of his eyes. Of course, he was the most handsome man she had ever seen. But somehow 'handsome' didn't have much relevance. Blade overcame regular features and stunning colouring by the sheer unyielding force of his personality.

As soon as she appeared at the door he took the tray from her, setting it down on the table with the unhurried courtesy she remembered. He waited until she was seated before he sat down, too. Sam Rogers liked that; she saw the approbation in his faded eyes.

'Blade is thinking of buying Onemahutu,' he said, his clipped, autocratic voice betraying nothing to Eden's shocked glance.

Eden's hands trembled, but she handed Blade his cup and saucer without spilling the tea. 'Are you?' she murmured, not meeting his eyes. 'You're a brave man, Mr Hammond.'

'Blade,' he reminded her with a note of command in the even voice.

'Blade,' she repeated obediently, hiding with thick, long lashes the green gleam of anger that lit her eyes for an instant. 'And you must call me Eden.'

His smile was lazy, yet she was sure he recognised her annoyance, and was amused by it. 'A pretty name,' he drawled. 'I've often wondered where you got it.'

She lifted her brows. 'My mother was a romantic.' And it had been her father's surname.

'But you're not?'

'No,' she said, her tone leaving no doubt. She might have been once, as adolescents were romantic, but she had left dreams long behind. The years of struggle had purged her of all illusions.

'Then we should deal well together,' he told her, amusement glittering in the pale depths of his eyes, 'because I'm not romantic, either.'

'She's a good, sensible girl,' her grandfather intervened bluntly. 'She hasn't got her head stuffed full of nonsense like most girls of her age; she knows that life is full of compromises.'

Put like that, Eden didn't know that she agreed entirely, but she smiled at her grandfather and gave him his tea before picking up her own cup. He looked—alive again, she thought sadly, stifling a flicker of ignoble jealousy. He hadn't looked so alert and interested since— oh, since her mother had died.

Apparently the prospect of selling Onemahutu wasn't worrying him at all! Had she been so mistaken in her presumptions?

'I want you to take Blade around,' Sam said, breaking in on her bewilderment. 'Saddle Thunderer, and show him the boundaries.'

'It's a long ride,' Eden remarked, wondering how she was going to get dinner on in time. She had planned a roast...

Blade's strong white teeth were revealed in a smile that understood her reservations. 'We don't have to go all the way around,' he said smoothly. 'I've flown over the place, so I know where the boundaries are. I just want to see the front paddocks. I'm staying in Kaikohe to-night, but——'

'Nonsense,' Sam interrupted firmly, 'you'll stay here. Best way of seeing it. You can ride out tonight and to-morrow morning, give yourself a much better look at the place.'

Eden smoothed out the tiny frown between her brows. But Blade Hammond had noticed. He was, she thought with resignation, altogether too perceptive.

'Can you stretch the meal?' he asked, his hard, beautiful mouth curling in a smile that warmed his eyes.

Her head came up. 'Yes,' she said simply. Of course she would have to make up one of the spare beds, take in the heater and air the room completely. Grandad wouldn't have thought of that, and she wasn't going to mention it. Onemahutu might look now like some back-country run-off, but it had a reputation for hospitality to uphold.

Silently listening to their conversation, she drank her tea, then waited a few minutes before saying, 'I've a few

things to do before we go riding, so if you'll excuse
me...?'

'Yes, of course,' Sam said impatiently. He was enjoying himself. Blade Hammond had a hard intelligence
that gave no quarter, and the older man was relishing
the quick thrust and parry of discussion. Eden firmly
squashed another pang that might have been resentment.

As soon as she moved, Blade got to his feet, taking
the tray from Eden's hands. 'Show me where to put it,'
he commanded.

She hesitated. 'It's all right, I'll do it.'

That vivid clear gaze dropped to the thin fragility of
her wrists. 'Where's the kitchen?'

Helpless before his resolute will, she went ahead. Once
in the big kitchen, modernised ten years ago when money
had been no object, Blade set the tray down on the
wooden bench, and looked around, but, although the
dark brows—brown, she noticed, not black—drew
together, she could discern no emotion in the handsome
face.

It wasn't, Eden deduced, that he didn't have emotions;
everyone did. At some stage of his life, probably in
childhood, Blade Hammond had learned that it was not
safe to reveal what he was feeling, and the habit had
stayed with him.

'Do you have any help here?' he asked.

Eden shook her head, hiding a bitter little smile. Seen
through his eyes, the kitchen must look as unkempt as
the rest of the house. She did her best, but it was more
important to expend her energy on the station than to
keep an immaculate house. It was an impossible job,
anyway, for one person. In the old days it had taken the
combined efforts of a housekeeper and her mother and
grandmother to keep it sparkling.

'I see.'

As he turned to go out, she found her voice. 'Mr
Hammond?' Suddenly lifted brows prompted her.

'Blade, I mean. Are you really thinking of buying Onemahutu?'

'Yes.'

She pressed her lips together, but she had to know. 'For what price?'

'That is something your grandfather and I have to discuss.'

It was said with perfect, if studied, courtesy, but she knew a snub when one came her way. Colour ran pinkly into her cheeks, but with the embarrassment came anger too, a spear of pure emotion that lit her eyes to incandescent emeralds. Unable to trust her voice, she nodded, but it wasn't until after he had left the room that she managed to unclench her fists. After all, he couldn't know that she had kept the books for the last two years. And that she needed to know what the price would be, so that she could start to make plans for some sort of future for herself and Sam.

But her stomach felt as though it had been kicked, because when all the debts had been paid she was sure there wasn't going to be enough to buy them a house. And if they couldn't do that . . .

Don't start worrying now, she told herself grimly, heading for the hallway. It may never happen! He could well take one horrified look at the neglected fences and pastures, and leave as abruptly as he had come.

After a quick, disheartening survey of the spare bedrooms, she decided to put Blade into the one next to hers because it was the only one that didn't reek of dampness and mildew. Old wooden houses needed constant attention to keep in good order, and Eden's best had not been good enough.

But the scent of the roses she picked in the garden dispelled some of the mustiness, and by the time she had put her electric blanket on the bed, and dusted then polished every wooden surface with lavender-scented beeswax, the room appeared less neglected. It, too, had been redecorated ten years ago with her grandmother's exquisite taste, so at least it looked superb.

Setting the heater on high, Eden wished that her grandfather had saved some of the money from the good years instead of spending it all, and even borrowing to put in dams and stockyards, sheds and races and air-strips, pour fertiliser on to the greedy ground, buy tractors and bulldozers. And entertain like a millionaire. Don't forget the trips around the world, she thought shamefacedly, for she had been on many of them.

Now, wife and daughter dead, himself unable to work, and wool and meat prices so far down that they'd left rock-bottom out of reach above them, Sam Rogers had to watch from the veranda of the homestead while weeds encroached with terrifying speed on to the expensive English grass in the paddocks. The sheds stood empty of fertiliser and machinery, and it was only by practising unrelenting economy that Eden found enough money to service the debts, with the barest amount left over to keep herself and Sam fed and clothed.

With a last look around the room, she left, and disappeared into the bathroom, showering quickly before pulling on fresh jeans and a faded but respectable shirt. She combed her wet hair out and, after a wistful glance at the hairdrier her mother had given her for her thirteenth birthday, left it to dry around her face. The hairdrier had given up the ghost a year ago.

That done, she prepared a rack of lamb and the vegetables to go with it, her brain as busy as her flying fingers. Leaving Onemahutu would be the biggest wrench in a lifetime made up of them, but Grandad had seemed almost cheerful about the prospect. Was he pretending, for her sake? She had learned to read his silences and his moods, and she knew that he fretted about her. If it eased his mind, she thought sadly, then she would smile as she drove out over the cattlestop for the last time.

Perhaps Blade Hammond, unlikely as it seemed, was an angel come to help them.

A spontaneous grin lit up her thin, solemn face at the thought of Blade Hammond as an angel. He had the right colouring, although there was a little too much red in that richly coloured hair to describe him as angelically fair. Certainly he was a creature of gold and light, from the burnished gold of his skin to the clear pale blue eyes.

A fallen angel, perhaps. In spite of his kindness Eden found him unnerving. Behind that intense male vitality he was so aloof, so self-contained, the real man hidden behind a façade of good looks and good manners.

Oh, stop it! she told herself crossly. You got over him five years ago! OK, so he's gorgeous-looking, and he's a very strong personality, but that doesn't mean you have to moon over him as though he's some rare, fascinating creature from outer space!

It had to be her lack of experience. Eden knew very little about men. She had been far too busy to go out with any of the men who asked her, and too exhausted to miss a social life. So after a while the men had stopped asking her out.

Not that she regretted the lack of invitations. A fine person she'd be, to go out at night and leave her grandfather to spend the long hours staring into the embers. It was bad enough during the daytime, although she tried to get in for morning and afternoon tea, and always came back for lunch.

If she knew more about men, perhaps she wouldn't find Blade Hammond so startling.

Blade! What sort of name was that for a grown man? she wondered, running outside to dig little new potatoes for dinner. As her fingers probed into the soft earth, warm now from the heat of the sun, she concluded that it was appropriate. He had a blade of a face, all angles and steel, the hard framework revealing that he would be handsome into his old age.

Back inside, she scrubbed the small white potatoes and put them in a pot with a sprig of mint, bringing them quickly to the boil before turning them off. For pudding she made apple snow, setting it to chill in the fridge.

Then she washed her hands and went back into the room she had prepared for Blade, turned the heater off, and checked that the electric blanket was airing the bed. The dankness was almost entirely gone, overcome by the sweet, erotic scent of the crimson roses in the cut-glass bowl. Ena Harkness, her grandmother's favourite. The bush was nearly dead, struggling gamely to survive neglect, but each spring and autumn it garlanded itself with the glowing blooms, the unbelievable perfume as richly sensual as the colour.

Last time Blade was there he had slept in the shearer's quarters down by the wool-shed, which were clean and comfortable but spartan. What had he been doing in the years since then?

Something that had earned him a small fortune; Onemahutu was run-down and neglected, but it was still worth a lot of money. And it would take him the equivalent of the purchase price to set it on its feet again. Now that banks were refusing to lend on any but the safest rural properties—which Onemahutu most certainly was not—he would need all of the purchase price in his pocket as well as the large sum necessary for development and re-stocking. So either he had a lot of cash, or an excellent credit rating. Or both.

Eden's brows drew together in a worried frown, but, as she came up the passage to the small room where her grandfather spent most of his days now, she heard him laugh with an appreciation and lack of restraint he hadn't shown for years. Her frown eased, to be replaced by a soft glow of love, tempered by resignation. To hear him laugh like that was worth anything.

She overcame the uncomfortable spark of envy, nailing her smile firmly to her wide mouth as she walked in through the door.

'Take Blade off now,' said her grandfather when he saw her. 'He wants to see as much of the place as he can before darkness.'

'All right. Is there anything I——?'

'No, no.' He was always testy when Eden made any reference to his disability. 'Off you go.'

She looked doubtfully at the man beside her. 'Do you want to change?'

'I've got leggings and boots in the car,' he told her calmly. 'That's all I need at the moment.'

'Go *on*!' Her grandfather frowned. 'Take him across the flats to the bottom hills and up the valley to Puketotara. He'll be able to see most of the place from there.'

'Yes, all right.' She dropped a kiss on his cheek, and went on out before Blade, her skin a little hot under his unwavering gaze.

She watched sharply as he mounted Thunderer, waiting for any sign that would reveal less than excellent horsemanship, but as soon as he swung into the saddle she relaxed. It was obvious even to the most inexpert onlooker that he was a man who had ridden from childhood. Lean hands gathered the reins, heavily muscled thighs gripped, showing the big black horse who was boss, and, after a few sideways steps, Thunderer accepted the man on his back as his master.

Eden leaned forward to pat Rusty's neck, and said, 'That's Puketotara up there,' nodding at the swelling bulk of the hill behind the homestead. 'If you like, we can go straight up. You get a good overview of most of Onemahutu from there. After that you can decide where else you want to go.'

'Yes, all right.' He clicked his tongue and the black horse lifted his ears, clearly looking forward to the ride ahead.

'You've been riding him, I take it?' Blade remarked after several minutes.

Eden's mouth tightened, but she nodded.

'He's too big for you,' he observed, his tone completely casual.

She said defensively, 'I know, but he's sweet-tempered, and someone has to ride him.'

'Your grandfather doesn't know?'

'No.' After a momentary hesitation she asked with awkward stiffness, 'Don't tell him, please. He'd only worry.'

'All right,' he agreed easily, 'I won't, if you promise not to ride the horse again.'

For a moment she didn't think she had heard right. Her head swung around and she stared up into eyes that were cool and bright and dispassionate. Her own kindled beneath that arrogant gaze. 'I don't think it's any of your business,' she said, oddly breathless yet determined not to show it.

'Perhaps not, but it is definitely your grandfather's.'

He was smiling, but she sensed the calm, implacable will beneath the golden surface, and realised that he meant every word he had said.

She bit her lip. At last, with immense reluctance, she said curtly, 'Very well, then.'

'I wonder, can you be trusted?' He laughed at the fulminating look she cast him, and leaned forward, bringing both their horses to a halt with a strong hand on Rusty's bridle. For a second he held her imprisoned in the trap of his survey, probing through the shields that self-discipline had imposed on her expression, until she had the strange sensation that he was able to see into her innermost soul. A sharp stab of sensation began at the base of her backbone and raced up her spine, to end astonishingly in a tight pulling feeling through her breasts.

'Yes, I think so,' he murmured, his eyes very blue, very confident.

He released the gelding then, leaving Eden shaken to her core, as though he had stirred up her personality and recreated it, transforming her into an entirely different person.

All the way up the steep track to the top of the hill she wondered just what had happened. Her senses were enhanced, her nerve-ends exposed as never before, so that the warm, familiar scent of grass and horses was more potent, the sunlight a thicker, richer gold, the gorse and manuka flowers glowing as they intermingled like gold and silver coins. The scent of the sea, wafting over the hills from the Hokianga harbour, tingled in her nostrils, and the skylark trilling with all the bravura of its species was casting shriller, sweeter, more brilliant cascades of delight than ever before into the clear air.

Even the tiredness that ached through her bones was overshadowed by an upwelling of anticipation, a keener edge to life than she had experienced for years.

Near the top of the hill the wind increased, tearing through the dark tangle of her hair. Eden pushed it back from her face, but it was too thick to control. Next time, she vowed, she'd remember to tie it back, or at least tether it under a scarf.

She looked across to see Blade Hammond watching her with an enigmatic expression that prickled her skin. Dismounting swiftly, she said, 'Y-you can let Thunderer go,' and was surprised, because she had expected this strange new mood to be evident in her voice, but it was just the same—oddly deep for such a small frame, a little husky. She was left-handed, and the involuntary hesitation was caused by an ill-advised attempt by her mother to get her to write right-handed. Linda Rogers had stopped as soon as she'd realised what was happening, but sometimes, when Eden was very tired or extremely emotional, that childhood stammer found its way back into her speech.

Blade nodded, and let the stallion free. Like Rusty, Thunderer immediately lowered his head to crop the grass. Jade sat down and scratched herself with vigour, dark eyes half closed.

'Grandad trained them himself,' Eden explained. 'He maintains that an animal you have to tie up every time you dismount is no use on a farm.'

'He's right.' Blade walked out to the edge of the hill, looking around him with a gaze that took in everything.

Standing beside him, Eden did the same, at first with the loving eyes of familiarity, then slowly, and with increasing unease, through his eyes. The grass was green, but the grass on the property next door had that particular velvety lushness that spoke of fertiliser and care. And across the paddocks, ugly as a rash, crept manuka and gorse and rushes and ragwort. For the past several years there hadn't been money to buy the sprays to control them.

She had been able to keep the fences in reasonably good order, but she was unable to replace posts, and in several places battens dipped suggestively. Rust showed through the paint on the sheds, and tarnished the roof of the homestead; grass poked up through the metal on the race that divided the property into four manageable segments.

Onemahutu was deteriorating. Each year that passed saw it sink further and further. If someone didn't rescue it soon it would take millions of dollars to restore it to productivity. The sheep were as healthy as she could keep them, but there had been no money for drenching this year, apart from the lambs, and they were showing it. She shuddered when she thought of the summer ahead, and the possibility of fly-strike. The cattle looked fit rather than sleek. There were not enough calves and lambs.

A bitter, painful sense of futility ate into Eden. For some obscure reason it hurt that it should be this man who gazed around and saw how little she had been able to accomplish, how feeble her efforts had been.

His deep, deliberate voice broke into her harried thoughts. 'Where's the boundary to the north?'

She pointed out the imaginary line on the crest of the blue bush-covered hills that separated Onemahutu from the Hokianga harbour. 'We're about halfway down the station,' she explained, turning. 'See that line of gum trees there? That's the southern boundary. We can't see the eastern one—it's well beyond those hills—but the western line is that row of tatty old macrocarpa trees, on the horizon behind those hills. You can just see them. Several were blown down in the last big wind we had, and they should all be cut down and a new shelter-belt planted.'

Another thing she hadn't done; when money was tight, trees were not a necessity. But those fallen macrocarpas had provided wood for their fires all last winter. Of necessity she had become proficient with a chain-saw and axe.

He nodded, keen eyes taking in everything, then whistled through his teeth. Thunderer's head came up; as he came towards them Eden's eyes filled with tears, the clear green smudged by dull brown.

'What is it?' Blade asked harshly.

His hand on her chin stopped the automatic, defensive sideways movement of Eden's face; she had to suffer that keen regard for several seconds until he let her go, but even as she ducked her face away he persisted, 'What's the matter, Eden?'

'I'm being s-silly.' Her voice was ragged and hesitant. Clearing her throat, she went on, 'Sorry. It's just that Grandad always called his horse like that. And now he'll never ride again.'

He slid his arm around her and gave her a brief, hard hug. 'The bloody unfairness of life,' he said harshly as he released her. 'He's been like that for a couple of years, hasn't he?'

'Yes.' She bit her lip, trying to stop it trembling, struggling to regain some composure so that she didn't blurt out her pain like a lost child. She had never told anyone what those years had been like, and it was strange that she should feel able to confide in this man she barely knew.

'I'm sorry,' she repeated, half under her breath. 'I don't normally go all silly over perfect strangers.'

'But I'm not a stranger,' he said, irony lending depth to his hard voice. 'You are a surprisingly self-contained creature for what, nineteen, is it now?'

The tears were blinked away now, the weakness gone. Carefully avoiding his gaze, she muttered, 'Yes.'

He nodded, but more as though it was confirmation of something he already knew, just as he had known of her grandfather's stroke. Eden suspected that Blade Hammond left very little to chance; he was a man who set goals and made sure he reached them. Something cold and apprehensive, some instinctive, primitive foreboding, pulled the hairs on her skin upright.

'What's over there?' he asked, his eyes going past her to the palings beneath the totara tree.

She hesitated, then explained, 'My mother. And my grandmother.'

'I see,' he said slowly, clear, compelling blue eyes moving from the small enclosure to her face, and back again. It was impossible to tell what he was thinking.

She nodded. For a moment she followed his gaze, then turned away. 'They both loved this view,' she said raggedly. 'Come on, Rusty, time to go home. Rusty, home!'

After swinging herself into the saddle, she waited while Thunderer settled down, admiring the effortless way Blade controlled the horse. He had good hands—light yet firm. They rode sedately down into the valley, Blade asking questions which she answered as accurately as she could.

'Do you still have workers here? I noticed that the cottages were occupied.'

She shook her head. 'No. Three of them are in excellent repair, so they're rented out, but the other one needs work done on it. The roof is leaking and there's something wrong with the plumbing.'

'I see.' His voice was distant, as though he was weighing something up.

She said quietly, 'Abe Rawhiri, in the first one, used to be a shepherd here. He's working a few miles down the road now as an odd-job man, but he's an excellent shepherd, and if you wanted to rehire him I'm sure he'd be happy to come back.'

Blade sent her a sharp, hard glance, then went back to gazing around, as though, she thought, halfway between resentment and misery, he already owned the place. The sun gleamed in the ripe amber waves of his hair, caught the hard-planed contours of his face. He looked magnificent, like a Viking sizing up a convent for plunder.

Something that was cold and hot at the same time worked its way up to the surface of Eden's skin. It was like a little buzz of sensation, exciting yet alarming. She thought that if anyone touched her now she might vibrate with some inner electricity. Rusty must have sensed it for he flicked his mane and an ear turned towards her.

'If he's so good, why didn't he get a job somewhere else?' Blade asked, his gaze moving to her face. 'Good shepherds are hard to find, and better paid than odd-job men.'

She had the ridiculous notion that he was testing her. 'His mother lives on the family marae a few miles away,' she said brusquely. 'She's old, and she wants to die there. Abe's her only child.'

He nodded, then looked away. It was almost as though he had released her. Her heart gave an odd thump as he remarked, 'The air-strip could be longer.'

'It's long enough for anything that flies around here.'

He lifted his brows but said nothing. Several lambs had found a little knoll, and were taking it in turns to play follow-my-leader, racing around to jump off the tiny bank, their tails quivering as they landed.

Eden laughed softly, unaware that Blade was watching her. 'I wonder how it feels to be airborne when you're a lamb?' she murmured.

'Much the same as it does when you're a human, I imagine. Have you ever done any sky-diving?'

Her eyes widened. 'No. Have you?'

'A couple of times.'

'What's it like?'

He grinned, teeth gleaming momentarily in the golden skin of his face. 'Like falling in love,' he said. 'Like living every moment of your life at once.'

Curiously she scanned his face, wondering why such a disciplined, deliberate man should enjoy such a reckless hobby. But in spite of the extravagant words his expression gave nothing away. She sighed. 'I went gliding once. It was lovely. Do you still jump?'

He was still smiling but the humour leached away. 'No,' he said. He must have noticed her barely restrained curiosity, for his mouth tightened, but he continued with no inflexion in his words, 'I have other ways of getting excitement now.'

Which left her completely unsatisfied, and wondering rather wildly why she was so curious about him.

# CHAPTER TWO

BACK at the house Blade carried the saddles and bridles into the barn, saying, as he hung them up, 'If it's too much trouble, I'll stay tonight in Kaikohe.'

Knowing that her grandfather would be horrified if she accepted this arrangement, Eden said swiftly, and, she hoped, convincingly, 'No, no, I've already made up your bed.'

'In that case I'll definitely accept your kind invitation.' Laughter lurked in the cool blue depths of his eyes, making her feel gauche and stupid.

The sweet scent of mock-orange blossom caught at her heart. With a bleak sense of desolation she looked around at the overgrown garden. Only the vegetable garden was cared for; in the borders, flowers fought with weeds, the husky intruders winning more often than not.

Once it had been beautiful, sweetly scented, a grafting of English garden know-how on to the vigour of this sub-tropical northland. Now it was a wilderness, but she loved it still, and it would tear her heart to shreds to leave it.

'If you'd like to bring in your suitcase, I'll show you where your room and the bathroom is,' she offered curtly. It was stupid to grieve. She would just have to face whatever the future brought with a head held high.

'I'll get it from the car,' he said.

Once inside, Eden removed the heater from his room, sniffing heartily to ensure that the last remnants of mustiness were completely gone. When she came out he was standing in the hall, a small case in his hand, looking at the painting of her grandmother as a young girl.

'I see where you get those eyes,' he startled her by saying.

She came to stand beside him, smiling a little wistfully. At seventeen, a year before she married, Dorothy Fernyhough had been exquisite, and the painter had responded to her shy child-into-woman mystery with sensitivity allied to great dramatic power. After he had painted her he had gone on to forge a brilliant career.

The portrait should have been sold when everything else had gone, but Eden hadn't even thought of it. It would be the last thing to go.

'She was beautiful,' she said softly. 'She was beautiful when she died. So was my mother.'

'Yes,' he replied deeply. 'I remember.'

Eden had forgotten that they had both been alive when he'd first come to Onemahutu. Something blurred her vision as she turned away.

'Your room's down here,' she told him, setting off down the passage. 'The bathroom's opposite. If there's anything you need, do tell me, won't you?'

He nodded, looking about him with interest as she opened the door. 'It looks very luxurious,' he said calmly. 'Thank you.'

Was he wondering why so much money had been spent on decorating the house? Eden flicked a look up at his face, but it revealed nothing, and she was glad to go out. A quick glance in at her grandfather showed him to have changed into a fresh shirt and jacket, and be sound asleep in his chair.

He slept more and more these days. The doctor said it was normal, that he was hoarding his strength, but it still alarmed her.

Tiptoeing out, she went down into the kitchen, washing her hands in what used to be the scullery before checking the roast and putting on the vegetables. Half an hour later she heard voices from the study, and hurried into the bathroom, walking warily, like a cat waiting for something unexpected to leap out at her.

But there was no sign that Blade Hammond had been there, apart from the damp air and a faint, slightly piny scent. Hastily she turned the taps on and got into the shower. As she soaped all over with the plain yellow soap which was all that she had been able to afford for two years, she wondered whether he really had any intention of buying Onemahutu.

Don't be so stupid, she scolded, recalling the strong angles of jaw and cheekbones, the clear, penetrating eyes, unwavering and arrogant—the face of a man who knew exactly what he was doing. Of course he planned to buy it.

How would leaving Onemahutu affect her grandfather? Surprisingly enough, he seemed almost eager to clinch the sale, but he was capable of putting on a good act to fool her. Eden knew—none better—that they could no longer go on like this. She had worked until she was so exhausted that she didn't even dream at night, but she was not able to keep it up, and worse than leaving was staying to watch the slow, inevitable deterioration. At least three men were needed to keep the station going, more if the place was to be restored to its previous productivity.

Frowning, her mind in a turmoil, she dried herself down and pulled on a dress, the only halfway decent one she had left. It was of fine wool in clear gold and peach shades, and it flattered her almost total lack of bosom with a gentle draping. Back in her bedroom, Eden looked objectively at herself, wondering why her genes had bestowed on her a lean, boyish, unfeminine, totally unromantic figure.

Even at seventeen, her grandmother had possessed more bosom than Eden had; grimacing at her reflection as she dragged a brush through her hair, she told herself scornfully that a D-cup bra and softly feminine flesh wouldn't get farm work done, but in her mind's eye she was seeing the sheer masculine appreciation that had been in Blade's eyes when he'd looked at the portrait.

Why should she be worrying about it now, when normally her lack of voluptuous appeal didn't enter her head?

With an impatient twitch of her shoulders, she left for the kitchen. Everything was well under control, so she walked along the passage to the study, her skin tingling with a tension she didn't understand.

'Ah, there you are, Eden.' Her grandfather smiled at her, whisky glass in his hand. It was, she noticed with a glance at the crystal decanter, his very best whisky—the stuff only brought out on important occasions.

But then, no doubt this was an important occasion.

'We've just been discussing the sale,' Sam said jovially, apparently not at all upset at the loss of the land he had given his life to. 'Blade's definitely going to buy.'

Eden managed to smile, although she thought dimly that it was the most difficult thing she had ever done. 'So you're celebrating,' she commented huskily.

Her eyes flashed automatically at the man who had stood up as she came into the room. He looked monumentally calm, she thought, not pleased or excited, not anything. Irrelevantly she wondered what it would take to pierce that impressive restraint.

'Yes, we're celebrating.' Her grandfather chuckled. 'Blade, can I ask you to pour some sherry for Eden?'

'Of course.' They seemed attuned, the old man and the young, in some way that cut her out. Trying not to resent it, she sat in her usual chair and watched through lowered lashes as Blade poured the drink, wondering why that broken nose, which should have marred his good looks, somehow saved them from being conventionally, boringly handsome. In some obscure way it added to his air of hard purposefulness.

Accepting the glass from him, she sipped at it, content to sit quietly as her grandfather asked, 'So, Blade, what persuaded you to give up the security of shearing and take your chances on the land?'

Blade's blue eyes were thoughtful as they scanned the old eagle countenance. 'I must be a gambler,' he said drily.

Eden's eyes widened. It was difficult to see Blade Hammond as a gambler. Difficult? No, it was almost impossible!

The older man's eyes were hooded as he looked back down the years. 'All life's a gamble. Where did you grow up?'

Blade Hammond smiled narrowly. 'On one of the big runs in the southern Alps; my mother was housekeeper at the homestead. That's where I learnt to sheer merinos, with a hand-blade. Which explains my nickname. My real name is Carl. When I was ten my mother sent me to boarding school in Nelson, but I wanted to own my own land, and the only way I could see to do that was to earn the money.' A smile with no amusement in it curled the corners of his mouth, not softening the hardness. 'When I left school I sat down and worked out a ten-year plan.'

Sam Rogers surveyed him shrewdly. 'So shearing was a way to earn good money quickly.'

'Yes.'

'I don't think I'd call you a gambler,' Sam said, genuine amusement lighting his faded eyes. 'And where do you go from here?'

That wide, hard mouth crooked. After a quick glance that Eden was sure scorched her face, Blade met the older man's gaze, his own brilliant and unreadable. 'I'm going to have to work out another ten-year plan,' he revealed non-committally.

Again Eden watched some sort of purely masculine message pass between the two men. But she was too strung up to make anything of it, or even to care. She sat quietly, trying to calm the chaotic turbulence of her emotions, where relief and an intense desolation fought for supremacy.

Her grandfather drank a little of his whisky then set the glass down. 'There's a lot of work to be done to get this place on its feet again. Eden has done her best, but it's far too much for one small girl, however hard she tries. And money; you'll need money. Make sure you don't get caught in the same trap I was, thinking the good days were going to last, and borrowing on the expectations of it.'

'No,' Blade Hammond said, his eyes moving to Eden's face, lingering there as she stared back, 'I have no intention of being caught in that trap.'

Her grandfather nodded. In a harsh voice he asked, 'So, when do you want us to go?'

Gently Blade swirled the amber liquid in his glass, considering, dark brows pulled together into a straight line. Eden thought that he was a man who took his time about all things—not in the least impetuous, perhaps more than a little calculating. He would have to be, to earn enough money to buy Onemahutu. He must have worked like a galley-slave and saved every cent he made.

Finally, looking at Eden with a cool watchfulness that sent a cold finger of ice down her spine, he said, 'I can see no reason why you should leave unless you want to. Not until you have found the right place for you to live. I'm going to be busy getting the place to rights, and I'd like the benefit of your expertise. If Eden feels like acting as housekeeper until such time as you get your affairs in order, I'll be grateful.'

Eden felt her grandfather's eyes on her face, but when she looked up he had already transferred his gaze to Blade's handsome, incommunicative countenance. 'I'd like that very much,' Sam said shortly.

Awkwardly, for she did not want to stay around Blade Hammond—he made her profoundly uncomfortable— Eden said, 'That's very kind of you, but——'

'Nonsense, there are no buts,' Sam broke in crisply, the authority in his voice painfully unusual. 'We'll stay.'

Blade lifted his glass, his unfaltering eyes resting on Eden's averted face. 'Naturally I'll pay you a decent wage,' he said. 'We can deal with that later. But, in the interim, I think we should drink to Onemahutu.'

They lifted their glasses and drank, Eden still torn by that unbearable mixture of emotions, unable to know whether she was happy or sad, or just plain exhausted.

The rest of the evening passed quietly. But, once in her bed, Eden did not crash to sleep immediately as she normally did. Instead, she lay staring out through the double-hung windows across the veranda to where the shaggy fronds of the huge Canary Island palm made emphatic statements across an improbably large moon, and wondered what it was going to be like living at Onemahutu with Blade Hammond.

In spite of that curiously controlled exterior, he was, she thought, essentially a kind man. And a clever one. He must have realised immediately that her grandfather dreaded going, leaving behind the graves of the wife and daughter he had adored.

Blade had also realised, of course, that there had been no husband, no father for Eden, but he hadn't revealed any curiosity or undue interest. Innately gallant? she wondered with a faint smile. Or tactful, perhaps, if the two weren't synonyms for the same quality?

The father she had never known was dead, too, drowned in the warm seas of the tropical Pacific while the woman he had been going to marry carried the child of their loving.

Once her grandmother told her that something had died in her mother with his death, but to Eden Linda Rogers had always been wonderful—bold and bright and dauntless even when she was racked with pain by the disease that finally killed her.

What would she have thought of Blade Hammond? Carl Hammond suited him, but Blade suited him better, Eden thought, commanding her restless body to lie still. He was like a blade, sharp and shining and incisive, setting himself goals and slicing through impediments with a fierce will and a frightening determination.

When she was fourteen she used to sneak down to the wool-shed to watch him, awed by the strength that was more than physical—the calm, effortless authority that kept the shearers under control even though some of them were much older than he was. She would not like to cross him, she had decided then. Five years had not changed her mind. He possessed a cool force of character that was as enigmatic as it was obvious.

Smiling, dreaming, her hair tangled across her pillow in a flood of ash-brown silk, she drifted off to sleep.

Dawn arrived at the same time as an imperative summons from her alarm clock. Eyes still half closed, Eden tumbled out of bed and along the passage into the bathroom. Although her arms and back protested violently at their abuse of the day before, she washed her face and cleaned her teeth, intent only on getting a slice of toast and some coffee inside herself before milking the cow.

She was still yawning when she made her way out again, but her jaw dropped slackly when Blade Hammond came out of his door. Until that moment she had forgotten entirely that he was there, which explained why all she was wearing was an inadequate T-shirt that had definitely seen better days. He was clad in a dark blue dressing-gown and, as far as Eden's horrified eyes could tell in a hastily averted glance, nothing else.

He looked big enough to fill up the doorway, and disgustingly fit and alert for so early in the morning.

She felt the whip of his glance down her body like wildfire, suffering embarrassment and a queer kind of shame because now he knew about her inadequate breasts and her unfeminine body and legs, with the strong thighs and calves of a horsewoman.

'Good morning,' he said, laughter glimmering for a moment in the pale depths of his eyes.

'Good morning.' It came out perilously close to a snap.
'I have a few things to do,' she continued tightly, 'but
I'll be making breakfast in about an hour.'

'If you wait ten minutes, I'll help you.'

Eden pushed a hand through the cloud of her hair,
wishing that she had brushed it before she'd gone into
the bathroom. 'No, it's all right,' she said nervously,
edging towards her door.

'I'll be in the kitchen in ten minutes,' he told her. There
wasn't much expression in his voice, no overt command,
but instinct warned her that she'd better be waiting in
the kitchen when he arrived there.

'All right,' she returned hoarsely, sliding through her
door in a manner that must have looked as though she
was practising being an eel.

As she climbed into jeans so old they were almost
white, and dragged on a T-shirt and a red and blue
checked shirt, before covering the lot with a jersey that
had also seen much better days, she wondered despairingly why he had that unsettling effect on her. He made
her tingle in a way that was as unpleasant as it was exciting. He set her nerve-ends jumping, and she'd developed a stupid habit of forgetting to breathe when he
was in the same room.

All in all, she thought with a desperate contempt, she
was behaving exactly the same way she had five years
ago, when she hadn't known any better.

Last night she had dreamt of him, dreams that had
faded until she'd seen him in the passage, tall and lean,
the dressing-gown hiding very little of his powerful male
torso, and nothing of the long, powerfully muscled thighs
and legs. Now those dreams came back in full force, and
she blushed deeply and with great mortification as she
fumbled about, trying to tie her hair back from her face
with an old bootlace.

How dared he invade her mind like that? And in such
a manner? They had been obscene, those dreams, especially as she had never in her life done that sort of

thing with any man. And she didn't want to do them with him, either, even if he did make her heart skip and flutter!

Once in the kitchen, she set the coffee to percolating, and put two slices of wholemeal bread into the toaster. Sure enough, almost exactly ten minutes later, he came in through the door, clad in a pair of moleskin trousers that, like hers, were far from new, and a dark blue cotton shirt with the sleeves rolled up beyond the elbow to reveal muscles that showed the effects of long hours spent in manual labour.

Her nerves began to hum. She poured coffee, asking in a muted voice, 'How do you have it?'

'With milk. No toast, thanks.'

He sounded amused, as though he recognised the turmoil he was causing in her, and found it mildly entertaining.

Irritation simmered deep within Eden, almost masking the puzzling sensations that tiptoed down her spine to coalesce in the pit of her stomach. After pouring milk into the cup, she pushed it across the huge kauri table, its wooden top white from countless scrubbings.

'Thank you,' he said calmly.

Mug in hand, she moved across to the old double-hung window, staring out at the perfect sight a double flowering crab-apple made as it held its blossoms up to the rising rays of the sun. Sudden tears blinded her. Yesterday everything had been easy; oh, it had been hard, back-breaking work, and she had been worried sick, but she could cope with that, she knew what she was doing. All she had to do was keep going, survive each long, punishing day.

Then Blade had driven in, like the calm centre of a hurricane, and suddenly none of the rules applied any longer. She was lost in a shifting, changing world, assailed by mutant emotions; she no longer recognised herself, and the cause of all of it was standing drinking coffee in the soft morning light, totally confident.

Next year the blossoms on her mother's crab-apple might well be just a memory for her. A hollow emptiness made her blink and hastily gulp down the rest of the coffee. What on earth was she going to do if things didn't work out here and he asked them to move on after a few months?

She had no talents, no skills except farming and housekeeping, and jobs were hard to come by even for people with good qualifications. What would she do?

Unconsciously Eden squared her shoulders. She had no idea how much money was going to be left when her grandfather had paid off all the debts, but perhaps there would be enough to buy a small house somewhere. And she could work. She wasn't proud; any job would do provided she earned enough to keep herself and her grandfather.

A touch on her shoulder made her gasp and whirl around, then wince as her sore muscles protested. For a big man, Blade moved surprisingly quietly. And he was too close. Rubbing the back of her neck, she moved a step away.

'Steady,' he said, looking at her with those eyes that were at the same time crystal-clear and curiously opaque. He watched her hand, his brows drawing together. 'What were you doing yesterday? You look as though every movement is exquisitely painful.'

Eden bit her lip, feeling an awful fool. 'I drenched the calves, but I'm all right—I just caught it the wrong way.'

She knew she couldn't feel the warmth emanating from him, but she was certainly far too hot. As she moved another step back in involuntary retreat, he asked, 'How many?'

She told him, and the frown intensified, but he made no comment, asking only, 'What do you do now?'

'I milk the cow, feed the dogs and the hens, work in the garden before the sun gets too hot...'

'I get the picture,' he said. 'I'll milk the cow.'

'You?' She stared at him in astonishment. He might be dressed in working clothes, but he carried himself with an unconscious arrogance that made her assume he wasn't accustomed to such menial labour as milking.

'Yes.' He gave her a narrow, almost taunting smile. 'I grew up on a place like this, Eden, only much more isolated. We were almost entirely self-sufficient. I can turn my hand to anything, and that includes making cheese and shoeing the horses.'

Feeling foolish, she went across to rinse out her mug. 'OK. The cow, Sweetheart, is really quiet, so you won't have any trouble with her. She'll stand to be milked. I'll do the hens and the dogs.'

'Do you only milk her once a day, or did you slip out last night?'

'I milk her in the morning. Eru, one of Abe's sons, milks her at night. They take all the spare milk too, to give to their pig. When they kill it they pay us with a ham.' She looked up at him, her eyes suddenly questioning. 'I hope they'll still be able to do that?'

Blade lifted his brows, but nodded. 'I can't see why not. Right, come and show me where everything is.'

He met her again half an hour later with a brimming bucket of milk in his hands. 'What do you want to do with this?'

'It goes into the cool-room. Here, give it to me——'

'It's too heavy,' he said, calmly walking past her. 'Where's the cool-room?'

Stalking ahead of him, she showed him the refrigerated room, its shelves almost empty now except for the few vegetables she had managed to freeze from the garden, and watched mutinously while he poured the milk into the pans, her eyes caught by the muscles that coiled in his shoulders and back as he lifted the heavy bucket with far less effort than she did.

The first time she had really appreciated the difference between men and women had been five years ago. She could see him now as plainly as though it had been only yesterday, muscles flexing beneath burnished skin as he moved with the effortless masculine strength she realised she was never going to be able to aspire to because she was the wrong sex.

It just didn't seem fair that every morning she had had to struggle to get the bucket up whereas he could manoeuvre it with such casual ease.

'Right,' he said over his shoulder, catching her watching him. The steady self-possession in his gaze altered; she thought she saw something darken in their depths, but he turned back again before she could be sure, and certainly his voice was even enough when he asked, 'What next?'

'The vegetable garden.' Eden's stomach was oddly hollow, as though she had just dropped several hundred feet in an air-pocket. She took the bucket from him, and went to scrub and scald it, her hands shaking a little while she tried to work out what on earth was the matter with her. She had seen men before, she thought feverishly, and none of them had made her feel like this.

But of course this was a continuation of that long-ago crush, and she wasn't handling it too well. Her back straightened. Well, she would learn to cope with it. She was not some adolescent, all hormones and insecurity; she was a grown woman, and, even though her body was playing her false, she could overcome that. She had to, because there was no future in it; she might be totally inexperienced, but she could read withdrawal, and that was what had been in Blade's eyes, in the calm, strong beauty of his face when he had seen her watching the play of muscles in his back and shoulder with avid appreciation.

He would not tell her so, because he was considerate, but he would make sure that she didn't get any stupid ideas about him. Perhaps he had a girlfriend—of course he must; he was a potent male animal, and she was certainly not the only woman to look at him and fantasise about delicious, forbidden things.

Last night, talking with Blade about his plans for Onemahutu, Grandad had been more alive, more his old self, than he had been since Gran's death. It was as though he had given up, and then Blade had come along like some agent of rejuvenation, offering him the opportunity to see his beloved Onemahutu come back to life. For that Eden would do anything; and, surely, controlling this damned inconvenient crush had to become easier with time?

'By the way,' Blade asked from the doorway, 'whose is that old rattle-trap out in the implement shed?'

She gave the bucket a final rinse, swirled the water competently around and tipped it down the tub, then set the bucket upside-down on the bench to dry. 'Ours,' she said composedly as she dried her hands. 'Yours, I suppose, as soon as you sign the papers.'

He was buying the station as a going concern, so everything—animals, equipment and machinery, were included in the purchase price.

His brows drew together. 'I don't think I'm going to like the answer to this, but I'd better have it anyway. I assume it's pensioned off, and is quietly and inexorably rotting into the ground?'

Eden shot him a turbulent look. 'No,' she said brusquely, walking up to the doorway.

He stood aside to let her through, but followed as she went out into the still, glorious day. 'You still drive it?'

Beneath the unruffled coolness of his voice Eden thought she discerned anger, and for some perverse reason she was pleased. That impervious control really exasperated her. Even to herself she refused to admit that it also frightened her.

'If I have to.' She bent and straightened her gumboots, sliding into them.

'Wait a minute,' he said dangerously as she started off down the path.

Eden despised herself, but the tone of his voice, the silky-soft warning, stopped her in mid-stride. The hair on the back of her neck lifted. 'What?' she asked, keeping her face resolutely turned away from him. One of the half-tame blackbirds that infested the homestead gardens hopped across the lawn in front of her, then, no doubt appreciating the tension, flew shrieking into the shrubs. Sensible bird.

'It hasn't got a warrant of fitness,' Blade said, still in that calm, level voice.

Eden shrugged.

'Eden, turn around.'

She took a deep breath, but turned, veiling her taut apprehension with her lashes. In spite of the electric atmosphere he looked the same as ever—imperturbable, the sun gleaming golden over the mask of his features.

'That's better,' he said approvingly, his eyes never leaving her face. 'You have an elegant, straight, and very eloquent back, but I'd rather see your face when I talk to you. You are not to get into that wretched wreck any more, do you understand? If you want to go anywhere you can take mine.'

'Yours?' she said stupidly.

He smiled, taking his time about it. 'After I've seen you drive, of course. Come on; you can show me how well you manage these roads.'

'Now?'

He must have thought she was a half-wit, but although his smile broadened there was no irritation in his expression. 'Yes, now,' he confirmed, explaining with gentle mockery, 'while there's no traffic on the road.'

His car was not new, nor was it old. It was well chosen for back-country roads with their uneven surfaces, being large, and higher off the road than most. In spite of power-steering it was heavy to manoeuvre, but Eden was accustomed to much worse. He hadn't overstated the case when he'd referred to the old utility as a wreck.

Of course she made some stupid mistakes as she drove down the road, grinding the gears a couple of times, once steering them into the ridge of gravel along the

verge, but she managed the skid well, and he didn't even
wince.

He would have been an excellent teacher, she thought,
irrationally petulant as he told her to pull into the council
metal-dump on the corner where their side-road de-
bouched on to the tarsealed highway. Patient, restrained, he praised her when she had done something
properly, instead of just criticising her mistakes, as so
many people did.

'This is a good place to practise backing,' he said.

Eden's hands were damp on the wheel. As she backed
between the big heaps of road metal, she noted the soft
green growth on the huge weeping willow on one side,
and the others that grew up the little stream behind it.
Yes, summer was almost here.

Where would she be next summer?

'Right, that's fine. Take us home again.'

On the way they met a big double-storeyed cattle truck
towing an equally large trailer, and, as she negotiated
the corner, Eden discovered how much more responsive
the car was than the old utility.

'Good,' Blade said calmly, apparently not at all
bothered by the closeness of the trailer as it swung around
the corner. 'You drive well. He was going too fast, but
you managed to get us out of his path without skidding
in the gravel. You can take the car any time you want
it, although talk it over with me before you go, will you,
as I'll probably have stuff to pick up in town most days?'

She had to ask. 'What if I do something stupid in it?'

He turned his head and smiled at her with some irony.
'I'll almost certainly be exceedingly rude, but don't worry
about it. We'll face any such problem when we come to
it.'

'Thank you,' she said politely, sounding like a well-
brought-up child.

'I have to leave after lunch,' he went on, watching her
with unnerving concentration. 'Do I have your promise
not to drive that impossible old wreck while I'm away?'

Her lips tightened. 'We have no other means of transport,' she told him tonelessly, 'and Grandad has to go to the doctor next week.'

'Is there a taxi in town?'

'Yes, but——'

Inflexibly he interrupted, 'Whatever reason you had for risking your grandfather—and yourself—in that thing no longer applies, does it?'

He meant that they would have money now that he was going to buy the station. What he couldn't know— no one except the accountant and the bank knew—was the extent of their debt. Well, what he didn't know about wasn't going to affect him. That was their problem.

'No,' she said quietly, hoping he would read it as capitulation.

But he was inexorable. 'So do I have your promise?'

She bit her lip.

'Eden?'

She nodded, feeling a heel, the worst sort of liar, for of course she was going to use the old van. Until she had some idea of how much money was going to be left after the debts were paid, she would have to keep econ-omising as rigidly as ever before. 'When will you be back?' she asked, hastily changing the subject in case he could read her falsehood in her voice or expression.

'Should be within a fortnight. I'll let you know well in advance.'

A fortnight. It was like a reprieve, yet never had a fortnight stretched so far ahead.

The confusion in her emotions angered her, so she spent the rest of the day being politely distant. It wasn't difficult, as Blade was closeted with her grandfather all morning, much of the time on the telephone, ringing through to Auckland a couple of times, and once to their local solicitor, who appeared on the doorstep half an hour later.

While the visitor conferred with Sam, Blade helped Eden get lunch. He seemed to understand her helpless frustration at being banished from the conclaves, for he explained what was happening. He was kind, Eden thought despairingly. Why couldn't he be—unthinking, so that she could get over this damned crush more quickly?

And he moved fast. By the end of the day Onemahutu was well on the way to becoming his.

When he finally left in his big car Eden was more than pleased to see him go.

But from then on all her grandfather could talk about was the reawakening of his beloved station, and she had to participate in case he wondered why she wasn't more enthusiastic. He spoke excitedly of Onemahutu, of Blade's plans, of how wonderful it was going to be to see them come to fruition. Eden joined in, hiding the tension that set every nerve in her body crossways.

One night, as she sat mending a pair of denim shorts, Sam asked abruptly, 'You like him, don't you?'

'Yes.' Her voice was muted, and she cleared her throat before adding a little too heartily, 'Very much.'

'Good.' He seemed to fall into a doze, but when Eden looked up she realised he was watching her. She smiled, the lovely warm smile she kept only for those she loved, and he blinked. 'That's the sort of man I'd like for you,' he said gruffly.

'Taken aback, she stared at him, colour rising through her transparent skin. 'Well—he's a bit old,' she commented idiotically.

'Plenty of women marry men eight years older than themselves. And you need a strong man; you can be a little spitfire when you're not too tired to think. Once I go you'll have no one left to take care of you.'

Eden hated it when he referred to his death. Subduing a clutch of fear, she stabbed the needle through the denim and expostulated, 'Women don't need to be looked after now, Grandad. We're independent!'

'A load of rubbish!' he retorted. 'Women are weaker than men; they need a man to care for them—at least while they're having the babies.'

She thought of having Blade's babies and felt a strange liquefying in the pit of her stomach, but she countered, 'Nonsense! Not nowadays, anyway. Men have become almost redundant in the world today!'

But, although her grandfather would normally have responded to such blatant provocation with a salty argument, he refused to rise to this bait. Instead he said, 'I would like to think that someone of my blood was here on Onemahutu when I'm gone.'

Now she understood. Gently, because she loved him, she said, 'Grandad, I don't think Blade sees me like that.'

'He sees a pretty, well-behaved girl,' he persisted obstinately. 'One who understands how important the land is, one who knows how to run a household this size, but, more importantly, he sees a lady—the right sort of woman for him to marry.'

She bit her lip. 'You loved Gran. Don't you want that for me, too?'

He said shortly, 'Love comes after the wedding, not before. It's not usually love that drives a man to propose; it's flash and dazzle. Love comes from sharing your life, growing together, living together.'

'Is that how it happened with you?' Eden was inexorable. She was going to stop this alarming attempt to matchmake right now.

'Yes. Oh, I thought I loved her when we were married, but it was nothing compared to how I grew to feel.' Flakes of colour lined his sharp cheekbones. 'Blade's a good man, Eden. You'd be safe with him.'

She put the shorts down, and sat at his feet as she used to when she was a small child. 'Yes, I know, but I don't want to feel that any man would marry me because he thinks I'd be the right sort of wife,' she said, laying her cheek on his knees. 'I want the flash and the dazzle as well, Grandad. I'd like to think that there is someone of Rogers blood at Onemahutu, too, but not if it means I have to sacrifice my life for it.'

'Would it be such a sacrifice?'

She hardened her heart. 'I think it would be.' Not to marry Blade, she thought wearily, not if he loved her. But her blood ran cold at the thought of being married for her usefulness, or because he felt sorry for her.

Sam's hand tightened, then cupped her face, and the other came to stroke across the cool flood of her hair. 'I feel that I've failed you,' he said painfully.

Her heart stopped. She turned her face and kissed his hand. 'Don't ever let me hear you say that again,' she remonstrated fiercely. 'Don't ever even think it. You love me, and if that was all you'd ever done for me it would be enough, but you've given me so much more. We've had bad times, but we were never promised milk and honey for life, were we?'

'No,' he said, his voice a little shaky.

'You don't need to worry about finding someone to take care of me, Grandad. And you have not failed me. If there is only one thing I've learned from growing up with you, it's how a gentleman behaves. That's quite a legacy to give anyone!'

He was silent, but when she looked up she saw him smiling. 'I think that's probably the greatest compliment I've ever had,' he said at last, unevenly. 'All right, I won't worry about you. But if Blade should show an interest in you, you won't turn him down just because of some bee in your bonnet about flash and dazzle, will you?'

It was important to him, so Eden pulled herself up and kissed his cheek. 'No, I won't,' she promised, knowing in her heart that Blade was never going to take that sort of interest in her. At least she had put a stop to any sort of matchmaking on her grandfather's part, she hoped. But her heart ached at his desire to leave some part of himself on Onemahutu.

She tried to ease it by cleaning the house out in between looking after the stock, wearing herself out so that she slept solidly at night without any impertinent dreams to make her blush the next day. Generally, she succeeded.

Blade, however, intruded too often into her life. When she came to take her grandfather to his appointment with the doctor the utility wouldn't start. A little probing revealed that someone had removed the rotor arm from the engine. Made savagely angry by the fact that Blade had read her so easily, Eden stamped into the house to ring up the local taxi, muttering about domineering, bossy, high-handed dictators.

Blade's personality must have had an equivalent impact on the notorious slowness of solicitors, for a week later everything was signed and sealed, and Onemahutu passed officially into his keeping.

Two days after that he arrived back at Onemahutu with two suitcases and a tea-chest, which apparently contained all his worldly goods. With him came a small gnarled man who smoked hand-rolled cigarettes and was introduced as Paul Trentham, the new cowman and gardener.

'Come in, Mr Trentham,' Eden said, smiling, because there was something inherently impudent in the glinting grey eyes that surveyed her so frankly. 'I haven't got a room ready——'

'No need to put me up,' he cut in. 'I'll camp in the house that's empty.'

'You can't. The plumbing needs repairs.'

'Makes no odds——' he began, but Eden interposed firmly.

'It won't take me more than ten minutes to make up a bed for you, so bring your gear in and leave it in the hall, and I'll make you a cup of tea straight away. You must both be thirsty; it's a really hot day.'

He cast a glance up at Blade, who, straight-faced, nodded. Grinning, Paul said, 'Right y'are, miss.'

'My name is Eden,' she told him, leading the way into the kitchen.

He chuckled. 'No milk in me tea, then, Eden.'

She didn't look at Blade, although she was acutely aware of his presence. Instead she talked to Paul, listening as he told her of the tiring trip up, stuck for a fair amount of the time behind cattle trucks and buses, and how things had changed since he was last in Northland forty years ago.

'Good driving got us here, though,' he finished. 'Blade here saved us a coupla times—once from some idiot in a fancy car who thought he could overtake a tanker on a corner. Good hands, Blade's got, on the reins or a wheel, and he got us out of that. Thought me last days had come.' He chuckled again. 'Mind you, so did the bloke in the little red car. Looked like a canary that'd come eye to eye with a tiger. Serves him bloo-blinkin' right, too.'

Eden's soft, husky laugh brought an answering grin to his old-young face. After she had poured the tea she went off to make up a bed in one of the spare rooms. Yesterday she had hauled all the mattresses out on to the veranda and let them bake in the sun; now they were sweet-smelling and completely aired. Smugly congratulating herself on her foresight, she dusted, and put out towels. Unfortunately they were not in as good shape as the mattresses. Her smile fading, she looked distastefully down at the threadbare one in her hand, and realised that she was going to have to ask Blade for money to replace quite a bit of linen.

At least her grandmother's sheets and tablecloths were the sort that lasted for centuries.

That evening she left the three men talking in the study, and went out on to the veranda, looking out across the valley as she grappled with ways of asking just what the domestic arrangements were going to be. A thin veil of cloud lessened the contrast between sky and stars, but even as she watched the cloud moved slowly north and dissipated, revealing the stars in their sparkling boldness, the old constellations of the northern hemisphere wheeling in the same slow synchronisation as the new, less well-known ones of the south.

Cold tendrils of unease pulled at Eden, adding to the inchoate, uncomfortable emotions struggling for supremacy inside her. Unknown tides and forces were at work in her life.

'I'm sorry I sprang Paul on you.'

Not normally easily startled, she jumped at the sound of Blade's voice. He had come out to the open french windows, and was standing there, dwarfing the opening.

'You didn't spring him on me,' she said after an unnerved moment. 'This is your house now; you're entitled to ask whoever you like here.'

He moved, quietly for such a big man, over the wooden floor of the veranda. 'Not without letting you know, I promise you. Eden, we haven't discussed your position here at all. Is this what you want?'

There could be only one answer to that. 'Yes,' she said, not really lying because she could not take her grandfather away.

Another silence, heavy with unspoken thoughts. 'Very well,' he said, the deep voice measured. 'Just do the things you normally did when you owned Onemahutu, but you take the weekends off completely. How does this sound for a salary?' He named a sum that made her blink.

'But that's far too much!' she exclaimed. 'Grandad—I mean, we'll both be living here!'

'It's going to be hard work.'

She hesitated, trying to stare through the darkness to gauge his expression, but it was impossible. After a moment she nodded. He was too pragmatic to pay her more than she was worth, and on such a salary she could save quickly. 'Thank you,' she murmured softly.

'I'll give you an allowance for household expenses, and we'll see how that works out. I'll give you a grant for whatever extra equipment you need to buy, as well.'

She gave a silent sigh of relief. Of course she should have expected him to have come up with something—he seemed to be a mind-reader but she realised that he was merely a very methodical man.

'Is Rusty your own horse? If he was bought for you, then you must keep him, and I'll buy another.'

He was being incredibly generous. Eden's hands tightened for a moment on the wooden veranda-rail. 'No, he's a stock horse,' she revealed in a muted voice. 'My horse was sold.'

'I see.'

Yes, of course he saw. Everything that didn't earn its keep had been sold. Sweet, spirited Fancy-Free had brought in a good sum.

'How long will it be before the workers arrive?' she asked on a rush, retreating from the bad memories.

'Abe Rawhiri starts tomorrow. I can manage with Paul and Abe until I buy in more stock, anyway.'

'I'd like to help if I can,' she said huskily.

He started to say something and then stopped. Looking up, she saw a flash of white as he smiled, and when he spoke his voice was crisp with irony. 'I was going to say that we can manage—I don't want you working too hard, but I don't suppose you'll work any harder than you have been. OK, if I need you I'll let you know.'

She clenched her hands on the balustrade, but she had decided that she had to say this. 'Thank you for suggesting we stay,' she said quietly, trying to steady her voice. 'It was a kind thing to do. Grandad didn't want to leave. But if we get in your way, you must tell us, please, and we'll go.' A note of unconscious pride coloured her voice.

'I doubt——'

'Please.'

His large hard hand came out and covered her cold ones in a warm grip.

'All right,' he agreed calmly. 'But I'm getting something from this arrangement too, don't forget. Your knowledge of the station will be invaluable, and I get an excellent housekeeper and a superb cook as well. Now, can you make a list of every repair that needs to be done around the place? Including the cottages and the various sheds, of course.'

'Yes.' She swallowed, her throat suddenly dry, and was relieved when he removed his hand. 'I'll go and do it now,' she said huskily.

'Tomorrow will do.'

There was a note of amusement in the deep, calm voice that made her wince. He had the ability, she thought indignantly, to reduce her to the child who had had such an abject crush on him all those years before.

# CHAPTER THREE

BLADE certainly got things going, however. The next morning Paul helped Eden with the chores, then told her with cheerful offhandedness that from now on he'd do all the outside jobs.

'The boss said so.' He grinned. 'Always do as the boss says; you'll find it's a lot easier. Otherwise you'll just wear yourself down to splinters, because Blade always gets his own way. He's in the habit of it.'

So Eden spent the next few days spring cleaning the house, an activity that lasted until Blade came in one lunchtime and found her precariously balanced on the top rung of the rickety old step-ladder, cleaning carefully the exquisite plaster rose in the middle of the drawing-room ceiling.

He strode across to the step-ladder, and held it firmly. 'Get down,' he said in a perfectly pleasant voice, but she descended faster than she had climbed up.

He had been riding around the stock, and he smelt of sunlight and horse and sweat, potent as an aphrodisiac. Eden stepped back nervously when she reached the floor. His face was still and hard, quite impassive, but she felt his anger like a cloak of lightning about him.

'I don't want to see you up there again,' he told her remotely. 'Those steps are dangerous.'

'But——'

'Eden.'

She refused to be intimidated. 'I'm spring cleaning,' she pointed out. 'I've done it before, and it's perfectly safe. I'm very careful.'

'Stay off ladders.'

Her brows shot up, but he meant it. 'It's safe enough, Blade——'

'Don't be an idiot.' His mouth clamped into an austere line. 'Put that ladder on to the pile of stuff to go to the dump, and make sure a new one goes on the list. And when it arrives, get someone else to come in and do that.'

He impaled her with a level, implacable stare. The words 'high-handed', and 'dictatorial' came once more to mind, but Eden was learning when it was useless to protest. For some reason he had made up his mind, and she could see that she wasn't going to convince him.

'Very well,' she said with great dignity.

'This is far too big a place for you to be trying to put it in order yourself. Get some help.' Another order, delivered in a calmly judicious tone that warned her not to object to this, either.

'I thought——' She stopped, turning pink.

He looked down, a glimmer of amusement easing the tension. 'Come on, spit it out.'

Eden's shoulders moved a little uneasily. 'I thought you were trying to economise,' she said at last. He hadn't said so, but he checked the expenditure carefully, and she had heard him talking to her grandfather, working out the most economical way of doing things.

'No, but I have a rooted objection to wasting money. I earned it the hard way.' He scanned her flushed face and wide green-brown eyes. 'However, there's enough to get Onemahutu in order, and that includes the homestead,' he finished.

How did he earn that money? The question must have been written plainly in her countenance, for he grinned suddenly, his eyes kindling to warmth. 'I saved my wages, and traded in stocks and shares.'

She was impressed. 'Isn't that difficult, and risky?'

'Speculation is risky,' he said. 'I didn't speculate. As for trading, no, if you know what you're doing, you're all right. Fortunately I saw the crash coming. I was in Australia at the time, where there were more opportunities.'

'Did you shear there?'

'No.' He shrugged. 'I was working in one of the mining towns.'

Eden nodded, understanding at last. 'Where you worked like a galley-slave for prince's wages.'

'Yes. And saved and traded some more. When I got back to New Zealand I had enough money, with the added help of a legacy, to buy a property.'

'I'm impressed,' she said.

He flicked a piercing glance at her. 'Are you?'

'Yes. Not many men would have such determination.'

He smiled, but although his eyes didn't leave her face she thought he no longer saw her. 'Saving money's easy when you have an overriding ambition.'

Eden wasn't too sure of that. She had known people with burning ambitions who were incapable of the kind of single-minded effort it must have taken for Blade to get this far. Daringly she asked, 'And now you've achieved your aim——?'

'No,' he said calmly, 'I haven't achieved it yet. I still have something to work for.' The smile that touched his beautiful mouth was a mixture of cynicism and sardonic amusement. 'And no, I'm not going to tell you what it is. You've already persuaded me to talk far too much about myself.'

Which was surely a compliment? Eden closed her mouth, blushing slightly, for she had indeed been going to ask him just that, which was a definite cheek. Only in this mood he was so easy to talk to. At her stricken look he laughed, this time with real humour, and gave a tiny pull on the hair she had scraped back from her face in her usual pony-tail before he went out. Eden watched him go, admiring without volition his easy stride, that inherent masculine grace.

Mindful of his instructions, she rang around the district until she found two women who were prepared to help her clean the house, as well as one high-school boy who had finished his exams and enjoyed climbing ladders. He had to be coached in the correct way to deal with the fancifully moulded ceilings and their elaborate cornices and roses, but he soon learned.

As they made their progress through the house to the sound of workmen on the roof replacing rusty iron, and the pervasive smell of paint—for a crew mended doors and window-frames and then repainted the timber weatherboarding in fresh, glossy white—Eden couldn't help comparing Blade's lonely quest, his stubborn determination, with her grandfather's life. Sam Rogers was kind, honest and hardworking; he had been born with money and seen it all slip through his fingers.

Eden simply could not imagine that happening to Blade.

It shamed her to see how much repair work needed to be done on the homestead, but when at last the working crew moved on to the cottages she looked around with satisfaction. The big old house sparkled.

Blade still slept in the room next to hers, but at her grandfather's prompting she took him one evening along to the master bedroom. It was huge, with a bow window out on to the veranda.

'I thought you might like to move into here,' she said, surveying the exquisitely carved and proportioned Victorian furniture with her brows pulled straight.

'Does it make you nervous having me in the next room?'

Her head jerked around. An odd little smile pulled at the corners of his hard mouth.

'No,' she said hastily. 'No, it doesn't at all.'

His half-closed eyes gleamed. 'In that case,' he asked smoothly, 'why change things?'

She said uncertainly, 'You'll have more privacy here. It has its own bathroom—when Grandad had the house renovated ten years ago, he had one put in—and there's a dressing-room too.'

He looked around. 'I suppose privacy is important,' he said almost to himself, then, making up his mind with the speed she had come to expect from him, 'All right.'

'The furniture was made for the room,' she explained tentatively, 'but if you find it too heavy... I mean, it's yours now.'

Frowning, he surveyed the kauri furniture, golden and gleaming with the polish of almost a hundred years, at home in that room as no other furniture would be.

'The furniture and contents are still yours,' he said shortly. 'They didn't go with the house.'

'Then what will we do about it?'

'Leave it there for the time being.' He tossed the curt words over a broad shoulder as he turned to leave the room.

'Well?' Sam asked when they came back. 'What do you think?'

Blade looked suddenly tired. He leaned back in his chair and closed his eyes, a nerve flicking beside the beautifully moulded line of his mouth. 'Can we get that furniture out of the room?' he asked.

'I doubt it, unless you pull it apart.' His own expression impassive, Sam was looking keenly at the tough, handsome face of the man who now owned Onemahutu. 'If you like it, you might as well have it. It's always been there; it would be a shame to take it out of the room. It's too big for any modern house, even though it's not as clumsy as most Victorian furniture.'

Blade's wide shoulders lifted in a shrug. 'So be it,' he said, his tone ironic.

Eden looked anxiously at him. He seemed to be in a strange mood, almost bitter, as though he was being forced to face something he didn't like.

She was assailed by a sudden impulse to go across and cradle the sun-warmed head against her breasts, hold him tenderly until the tiredness seeped away from his magnificent body and she could feel the strength and vitality pour through him again.

Colour rioted up through her skin, touching it with rose, and she looked hastily away. She would have to control her stupid heart, the pulses that rocketed through her, the way her eyes smiled when they saw him, or he would know that she still had a crush on him. And this time he wouldn't treat her as he had five years ago, with a pleasant, distant courtesy. He would withdraw completely. She knew that there was no way he could return this passionate interest, but she wanted his friendship.

It would be something to be Blade Hammond's friend, she thought wistfully, sneaking another look at his shuttered face, just as he opened his eyes and caught her staring.

'I'll get the room ready for you tomorrow,' she said hastily, her tongue scrambling over the words.

His glance was coolly speculative as he scanned her face. 'OK, but I'll move my clothes myself.'

'Fine.' Stilted. She sounded stilted, just when she longed to sound composed and sure of herself, borrow a little of that impervious composure from him.

'Right, that's settled,' Sam said with something like satisfaction.

Blade frowned, the dark brows drawing together in a straight line above his broken nose. Eden said quickly, 'I won't climb the ladder. The room's already been cleaned, anyway.'

'Good,' he replied, holding her gaze a moment longer. 'I'll make a cup of tea, I think——'

'Eden can do that,' her grandfather broke in. 'I want to talk to you about that new line of beef you were thinking of getting—the Belgian Blues.'

Blade came into the kitchen just as she was setting out biscuits on a dish. He was wearing a casual pair of trousers and a blue shirt that intensified but didn't brighten the colour of his eyes, and he looked lean and potently dangerous.

'Mm,' he said, reaching out to scoop up one of the biscuits she had made that afternoon, 'you've been busy.'

'Anzac biscuits. They're Grandad's favourite.' She grinned at him. 'I can bake two cakes and three different biscuits. I have a very limited repertoire, but what I do, I do well.'

'You do indeed.' He demolished the biscuit then lifted the tray. 'Let's go, then.'

Sam was asleep, but, in spite of the fact that Eden stepped lightly and Blade made no noise at all, he woke the minute they came into the room. 'Just resting,' he told them, smiling sardonically. 'When a man gets to my age, he needs a little more rest.' He looked across at Eden. 'You should be off to bed too,' he told her. 'I saw you out digging in the garden in the middle of the day, you silly child.'

Blade's head turned slowly. 'You were what?'

She shrugged, cross with her grandfather, cross with Blade. The freedom she hadn't valued enough when she'd had it was being torpedoed, taken from her by over-protective men. 'The weeds die faster if you dig them,' she asserted defensively.

Blade said quietly, 'Digging is Paul's work.'

A sliver of ice slid the length of Eden's spine. 'He was out with you and Abe.'

He accepted a cup of tea from her, saying with an air of finality, 'Nevertheless, Sam is quite right; you shouldn't have been digging, and certainly not in the sun. No more. I forbid you to.'

Her brows shot up. 'Forbid?' she asked faintly.

He smiled at her with great certainty and immense, unaffected charm. 'Yes.' In that monosyllable was all the confidence in the world. Blade Hammond had forbidden it, and so it would be.

Anger sizzled along her nerve-ends, anger that was pure and hot and bright. Eden controlled it because common sense told her that, if she let go, he, with his superb control, would have her at a complete disadvantage.

'I suppose,' she began contemplatively, 'that if Grandad forbade me to do anything I might have to *listen*. But I should perhaps tell you that he is the only person I'd listen to, and even then I doubt whether I'd actually take any notice of him.'

Blade ignored Sam's snort. He scanned her mutinous face, then let his eyes wander down her body, steel-slim, blade-straight in her chair, vibrating with anger. He said calmly, 'You had better take notice of me. Or take the consequences.'

She was going to ask him what the consequences would be, when it suddenly occurred to her that he could be threatening her with the loss of the job he had promised her, and with it her grandfather's refuge.

Surely he would not be so brutal?

But ruthlessness was the other side of the determination she admired so. He had to be ruthless with himself and with anyone who got in his way, otherwise he would never have been able to accomplish what he had.

Eden's mouth tightened. She looked down blindly into the tea in her cup, realising that she couldn't tell him smartly where to get off. He could sack her if he felt like it.

It hurt; it really hurt, but she summoned the courage to look him levelly in the eye and say with as much fortitude as she could, 'Very well, then. You are my employer, after all.'

That made him frown, she was pleased to see, but almost instantly the frown faded and he smiled, a little lop-sidedly. 'I'm glad you realise it,' he said gently, and began to talk to Sam about haymaking.

Not tasting it, Eden drank her tea, then set the cup down. Her hand, she realised, was shaking slightly. He had put her very neatly in her place. There would be no friendship such as she had hoped for—only the sort of relationship there could be between a man and the woman he employed to keep his house clean and tidy.

She had been foolish, but it was over. At least her dreams had not seen the light of day; they had died stillborn, before she'd even understood that they were there.

When the tea had been drunk she put the cups back on the tray and carried it from the room, averting her head a little as Blade held the door open. Something new-born and vulnerable, something so budding and callow that she didn't even recognise it, had died, and she was too raw to be able to deal with it yet.

Once in the kitchen she washed up before checking to see that she had the ingredients for lunch the next day. A chicken salad, she had decided, opening the fridge door. In the pantry she found avocados, and small, tasty tomatoes and tiny new potatoes. She very carefully didn't think of Blade again. She had been shown the limits of her power and her influence, and she was a quick learner; she wouldn't need to be told again.

He complimented her on that lunch, as he complimented her on most of her meals. He was always gravely courteous, even, she thought with a pang, when he was pointing out that she was merely the hired hand. After lunch she settled down to do some ironing. Outside the golden day beckoned, but there was a pile of clothes that had to be coped with first. Blade and Abe and Paul were fencing.

Sighing, she plugged in. At least when she had been working her heart out on the farm she had been outside, she thought resentfully. Then she reminded herself with resigned honesty that then she'd always been exhausted, so tired that the sun was an enemy.

She spent an hour catching up on the ironing, biting her lip in some odd emotion as she dealt with the well-worn cotton shirts that Blade wore now that the weather was warm. His good clothes were expensively hand-made, probably because he was so big that the normal-sized wouldn't have fitted.

In many ways he was an enigma. It was impossible to tell what he was thinking unless he wanted her to. And although his mother had been a housekeeper he spoke like the son of the house, without any of the flattened vowel sounds that marked many New Zealanders' speech.

However, she mused, he was tidy, unlike her grand-father, whose knowledge of housekeeping was limited to the whereabouts of the clothes that appeared, im-maculately pressed, in his drawers and his wardrobe! Blade was accustomed to looking after himself. He made his bed every morning, and left both bedroom and bathroom tidy, clothes picked up, shoes put away.

The ironing done, she peeped in on her grandfather, who was asleep on his bed, then, with more than a hint of defiance in the set of her shoulders and chin, went out into the garden. However, she prudently chose to work beneath the wide, shady branches of the silk tree, safely out of the sun, tearing into the weeds, yanking them out with a ferocity she couldn't keep up for long without exhausting herself. But at least there was a sat-isfactory pile to be carried off to the compost heap, and when she came back in to make afternoon tea Grandad was up and about, reading the newspaper Blade had col-lected from the letter-box at the gate at lunchtime.

'You look hot,' he told her disapprovingly. 'And dirty. Been digging again?'

'No.' She smiled pertly as she bent to kiss his cheek. 'I've been weeding. In the shade.'

His chuckle followed her as she went off to shower. Anything, she thought urgently, anything at all would be worth it, just to hear him laugh like that. She hadn't realised how silent and depressed he had become over the past two years.

At five o'clock she had dinner cooking and everything under control. Indignant at her weakness, she still found herself listening for the sound of Thunderer's hoofs.

The telephone rang just as Blade strode in through the door. Eden picked up the receiver. 'Hello,' she said.

There was a moment's hesitation at the other end, then a rich feminine voice responded, 'And who might you be, I wonder?'

'Sorry?'

'I want to speak to Blade Hammond,' the woman stated, all laughter fled from the lovely tones. 'Is he there?'

'Yes,' Eden told her. 'He's just come in.' She held out the receiver, saying blandly, 'Someone for you, Blade.'

As she went back into the kitchen she heard him drawl with an amusement he made no attempt to hide, "Thea, you have no need to intimidate my housekeeper.' He chuckled, before answering what seemed to be a loud and extremely crisp comment. 'Really? I'm flattered...'

Eden slid some rosemary in with the lamb, feeling as though she had been hit in the stomach. Her mouth pulled into a straight line.

So her name was Thea. Elegant—a special name for a special woman. But then, any woman Blade Hammond was interested in would be a special woman because he was undoubtedly a special man. A virile, powerful man, with a potent masculine attraction that drew every woman's interested attention.

He was welcome to Thea Whoever-She-Was, Eden decided, using her anger at the woman's attitude to cover up a sinking desolation that yawned at her feet like a pit.

The woman was certainly interested in him. She rang several times a week, and, although her voice didn't exactly soften, she never subjected Eden to that sharp tone again. She even remembered her name, sometimes. Eden hated her.

But as the days lengthened towards summer, growing warmer even when it rained, which it did often enough to negate any thought of a drought, she became more confident. She was sure Blade had no idea that she was in the throes of a massive crush. He treated her with the casual kindness of an older brother, teasing her gently, making her laugh, talking to her with that unfaltering courtesy, only occasionally showing the steel beneath that golden mask.

Such as the time he found her in the garden one Sunday afternoon.

'What the hell are you doing?' he demanded without preamble.

She squatted back on her heels, giving him a pert look from beneath her lashes. 'As you see, I'm weeding. In the shade.'

Grabbing her by the shoulders, he used his enormous strength to lift her to her feet. 'Today is Sunday, which means that officially you are not working.'

'But the weather forecast says it's going to rain tomorrow.'

He squashed a bloodthirsty sandfly on her arm with detached gentleness. 'No. Go and read, or sunbathe, or something like that.'

Eden smiled. He was very kind, even when he was overbearing. 'I'll take time off tomorrow when it's raining,' she said in what she hoped was a sweetly reasonable tone, trying to ignore the little drum that beat in her throat.

'You suggested that ten days ago, remember? But you went on working inside the next day. You are entitled to time off.'

She shrugged, pulling away because it was sheer hell to be so close to him and know that he felt nothing of this wild excitement that licked through her body.

'I won't do that this time,' she promised, placating him. If she stopped working she had too much time to think.

He stood watching her from beneath frowning brows. 'Why don't you have any social life? I've been here a month, and you haven't gone anywhere.'

She moved her shoulders, made uneasy by that shrewd glance. 'I was always so busy,' she said quietly, 'I didn't have time to go out, and when I did I was too tired to enjoy myself. I'm out of touch with my age group, I suppose.'

His frown deepened, then smoothed away, but he stood silent for a moment, as though something unpleasant had occurred to him. 'You've had no real life at all, have you?' he said slowly. 'Go and get your togs, and I'll take you across to Paihia for a swim.'

'Swim?' She looked at him with horror. 'It's far too cold to swim yet! The water will be freezing.'

'Nonsense. The sea's at its warmest at this time of year.'

Temptation tasted sweet as a peach in her mouth, but she shook her head. 'It's lovely of you to ask, but I can't go. Grandad will be alone,' she explained quietly.

'He's not so dependent on you that you can't ever go out without him, surely?'

Shock stopped the tumbling words. She stared at him, and met shards of blue diamond. 'He's not dependent at all,' she said haughtily, her cheeks very flushed but her mouth set into a determined line.

'Then give him the chance to say whether he needs you or not.'

Sam said cheerfully, when she approached him, 'Of course I'll be all right; don't fuss, Eden. I'm going to have a little sleep, and then Enid Clare's coming over to bring some mail that wound up in their letter-box instead of ours, so off you go.' He smiled benignly at them both.

Aware of Blade's silent insistence, Eden hesitated for a second, then yielded. He was just being kind, she knew—perhaps he was even feeling a little sorry for her; but, even so, she wanted to go out with him, especially as it might only be this once. 'I won't be more than ten minutes,' she promised as she fled along to her bedroom.

Paihia, a beach resort in the exquisite Bay of Islands, was three-quarters of an hour away over roads that were, so Blade drily told Eden, seething with traffic compared to most South Island roads.

'What made you decide to come up here?' she asked. It was something that had been piquing her curiosity ever since he'd bought the station. 'Surely you'd have found farming in the South Island far more familiar than up here, where conditions are so different?'

A muscle flicked beside his mouth and, although his expression didn't alter, she had the sudden uneasy feeling that she had touched a tender spot. But his voice remained the same, cool and deep and imperturbable, when he replied, 'A good farmer is a good farmer anywhere. And Onemahutu was the right price.'

She nodded. 'I hope it's what you want,' she said shyly.

He slanted her an enigmatic glance. 'It's a start,' he replied. 'There'll be quite a few changes. I don't intend to leave it the way it is. It's too vulnerable, as you and your grandfather found out, to market forces. I think the future lies with mixed farms, far more intensively farmed than Onemahutu is at the moment.'

'A mixed farm?' She looked at him. 'It *is* mixed; it has sheep and cattle.'

'I don't mean like that. I'm going to subdivide the property, turn the divisions into self-supporting units with managers, and try a few experiments.'

'Such as?'

'Forestry, for one.'

'That will use up a lot of good grazing land,' she pointed out slowly.

'Not necessarily—not if the wood-lots are combined with grass, so that after the first several years cattle can be grazed beneath the trees. It's been done already in parts of Northland, and I can't see why it wouldn't work on Onemahutu.'

'Ah, agro-forestry. It's taking quite a chance,' she said doubtfully. 'And it's not a terribly good time, surely, for doing that?'

His mouth straightened into a pure, determined line. 'I try to cover every eventuality. Everything I start, I've planned and researched until I'm damned sure I can carry through. Some of my theories will work and some won't, but at least every one I try out will have a chance.'

Yes, she could believe that. He planned well ahead, this quiet, strong man with the blond good looks of a movie hero and the core of steel, the almost frightening determination. She dampened dry lips and began to talk of agro-forestry; the subject occupied them until they reached Paihia.

'Where's the best place to swim?' he asked.

'Turn left here.' She directed them down Waitangi beach and past the Maori marae—one of the best-known and most prestigious in the country. The warm weather had pulled out locals and tourists alike, and the beach was dotted with bodies lying on towels, trying to get a good start to the serious business of tanning carefully; but not many were swimming.

'See,' she pointed out smugly, 'the water is too cold.'

'Only for a pack of effete Northerners,' he returned, the corners of his mouth tucking in as they did when he was amused.

Suddenly carefree, pleasure fizzing in her like sherbet, Eden retorted, 'Of course in the South Island you swim among icebergs, don't you, with penguins diving in off the floes?'

'Almost invariably.' He pulled up as they came past the shipwreck museum—an old sugar barge with its masts restored—and waited by the one-way bridge over the Waitangi River for a Land Rover to come through. Many of the yachts and run-abouts moored in the river had gone out for the day, and more were being put in the water along at the ramp past the pohutukawa trees. The narrow wooden bridge already had two cars coming the opposite way, so they had to wait for them to get across.

Blade slanted her a mocking glance, his lashes hiding everything but a blue gleam of mischief in their depths. 'We have stamina, we mainlanders. And, although your water here may be warmer than ours ever gets, you Northerners don't know what heat is. Where I come from a hot day is thirty-five degrees, not the measly twenty-seven you puff and gasp and complain about here.'

Eden grinned, admitting defeat. 'OK, so we have a nice, temperate climate: no snow, no great heat, not much difference between summer and winter——'

'But plenty of humidity,' he retorted, driving on to the now empty bridge, 'and more than enough rain!'

'You shouldn't have come north if you didn't like a little humidity,' she said impudently, laughing at him through her lashes.

He smiled. 'I suppose not. It's not as though I didn't know, Northland being notorious for its sticky days and nights, and its lousy spring weather.'

'Come on, now,' she protested, determined not to let him get away with such a slight. 'The humidity's not that bad! And even if our springs are pretty wet, we do autumns really well.'

'All of New Zealand does autumn well,' he said, laughing at her indignant face. 'Now, where do you like to swim?'

'If you turn right here we can go through the yacht club grounds to the hotel beach. Grandad's a life member of the club, so we can use their facilities. The beach is not as good as the big one, but it's not so crowded, either.'

Which meant fewer people to stare at her faded, unfashionable swimsuit.

He turned the wheel and they drove beneath pines to the yacht club enclosure, parking on the grass on the other side of the clubhouse. Eden hopped out, pushing her hair back from her face. The sun danced on the water, the trees danced above them, and multi-coloured sails flirted and dipped across the surface of the bay. Elation expanded to fill her, lifting her from the thick green carpet of grass, so that she was new and re-made, a person who had never existed until that moment.

'I love the beach,' she confided impulsively as they walked across to the small crescent of sand in front of the hotel.

Blade slanted her a teasing look. 'But not swimming?'

She grinned. 'Oh, I like that, too, when the water's warm.'

'Wimp. Is that why the pool at the homestead isn't in use?'

'No, I used to be in it all the time when I was a kid. They had to drag me out, but in the end they realised that it wasn't going to hurt me. I was supposed to be delicate,' she said a little gruffly. 'Mum used to fuss about me overtaxing myself; I don't know why. I didn't go to school, not even to high school. Mum taught me at home with lessons from the correspondence school.'

'You don't appear delicate now.'

She was suddenly worried in case he thought she was too fragile to keep house for him. 'I'm not. I can work as hard as most men.'

'So I saw,' he said non-committally. They had reached the beach, and he looked around at the people on the sand, some sprawled flat on towels, some sitting in deck-chairs. Several women, Eden was embarrassed to see, were sunbathing topless, and behind the dark glasses many were watching the two newcomers.

Colour scorched through her clear skin, but almost immediately she realised that they were not in the least interested in her.

Swallowing fiercely, she ducked her head as Blade shed his shirt and shorts to reveal sleek dark blue trunks. The sun gleamed amber and gold in his hair, gilded his face and arms with its benison, highlighting the calm, sure strength of his features. Ignoring the onlookers, he stood gazing out over the glittering, restless waters of the bay, his big body relaxed, yet poised and alert. Where had he learned to be so—watchful? And how had he managed to acquire that utter self-containment, that air of being completely sufficient to himself?

Although he couldn't have seen it, Eden must have made some sort of movement, for he swung around and looked straight at her. She saw his smile, white in his face.

'Can I persuade you to swim now, or are you going to lie on the beach and work on your tan?' he asked, his tone as teasing as the question, but his bright blue eyes were guarded now.

She had given herself away. The only thing to do was pretend it hadn't happened. Eden managed to summon a smile. 'I suppose I'll have to,' she said jauntily, 'if only to prove that not all Northlanders are effete!'

He didn't watch while she stripped off her T-shirt and shorts. Beneath was the faded swimsuit she had worn since she was sixteen. Originally a pretty colour, it had faded to a dull, patchy blue which did nothing for her fine, pale skin. Not that she had any reason to be embarrassed. The watching eyes behind the dark glasses were fixed firmly on Blade, assessing the emphatic masculine lines of muscled thighs and calves, the purposeful male triangles of shoulder and hips, tight buttocks, and legs planted sightly apart in the yielding sand.

The sun irradiated the slightly darker dusting of body hair, so that he seemed to glow like a golden man, a fabled deity of some ancient pagan time—calm, sure, autocratically certain of his godhead and the privileges it entitled him to.

Beside him, in her old suit with her boyish body and thin face, Eden knew she must look like some ugly duckling. 'Let's go,' she said, self-consciousness making her voice thin and strained.

The water was quite warm, and she swam in her fairly primitive style for twenty minutes or so, taking care to keep away from Blade. He, of course, was an excellent swimmer, cutting smoothly and powerfully through the water.

Angry with him for being so impervious, but more with herself for being so aware of him, she splashed out of the water, picked up her clothes and towel, and strode off to change at the yacht club, prey to a bewildering range of emotions, the predominant one of which was sheer humiliating chagrin.

She had only just got under the shower when a woman's voice asked, 'Eden? Eden Rogers? Are you in there?'

'Yes,' she said, astonished. 'Who is it?'

The woman gave a slow laugh. 'Your boyfriend was worried; he didn't know where you were, so he asked if I'd check things out for him.'

'Boyfriend'? Sudden comprehension stole her wits. 'Oh! Oh, thanks. Thanks. Could you tell him I'll be out in a minute?'

'Certainly. I wouldn't leave him more than a minute, though, if I were you, in case someone snaffles him up. Men like that don't come along too often in a woman's life!' And, laughing, she went out.

Still seething with quite irrational anger, Eden took her time washing the salt from her hair, deliberately wallowing in the cool, fresh water. But at last she couldn't spin it out any longer, so she turned the shower off and stepped out, wondering savagely as she rubbed herself down with the towel whether she would find him talking to the sultry-voiced woman.

He certainly didn't appear to be waiting for her. As she came through the door her eyes flew to where he was standing in the middle of the club-room, talking to a man and a very interested woman. He too had showered, and was once more clad in the shirt and shorts, which gave an excellent view of broad shoulders and long, heavily muscled legs.

He had, Eden decided bleakly, some attention-grabbing quality that made him stand out wherever he was. It wasn't just that he was handsome, because the man he was talking to, Nick Stockley, a local landowner, was extremely good-looking, very rich, very well-connected, who didn't have half Blade's charisma. Although possessing the kind of body that was the epitome of masculinity no doubt helped, it wasn't that entirely, either. Other men had broad shoulders and narrow hips, long legs and lean, competent hands. In this farming district they almost all had muscles.

Perhaps it was the way he stood, balanced, arrogantly erect. Or the way he held his head. Or perhaps, Eden thought as she crossed the shiny wooden floor towards them, perhaps it was that aura of power, of potent male effectiveness, at once immensely reassuring and dangerous, based as it was on the more primal character traits that went back to the days when often the only thing that stood between a woman and death was the ability of her mate to deal with the threat.

In spite of the fact that he seemed to have his whole attention on Nick Stockley's sister, who was surveying him as though he were an extremely well-wrapped parcel with her name on it, Eden knew that Blade was aware of every step she took, and that he was angry with her.

As she came up Jan Stockley put her hand on his arm, letting the long pink nails trail lightly across his skin for a second as she laughed up into his face. She was very beautiful, very seductive.

Eden was clawed by jealousy each time she heard Thea's voice on the telephone, but Thea was safely at the other end of the line. The emotions that swamped her now were hard and raw and hot, horrifying in their intensity. She had always thought of herself as placid; now she realised that it was only because until Blade's arrival she had never been emotionally or physically affected by a man.

Her head came up. She even managed to smile. Blade's face was still impassive, but his eyes were like chips of blue ice.

'Hello, Eden.' As she stopped Nick hooked an arm around her shoulders and gave her a swift hug.

She knew him well. He called in as often as he could to see Sam, and always treated her with the casual affection of a man for his younger cousin, so she took both his hug and his million megawatt smile in her stride. He was probably the most eligible bachelor in Northland;

at least, Eden thought as she smiled back, he had been until Blade arrived.

'What can I get you to drink?' Nick asked as he released her.

'Nothing, thanks.' She waited until his sister dragged her reluctant eyes from Blade's face, then said coolly, 'Hello, Jan.'

In spite of his dangerous reputation Nick was a darling, which made it all the more surprising that Jan should be such a pain.

'Oh, Eden,' she said now, dismissively. 'You shouldn't wear pink, you know, especially not that bright pink. Why don't you get your colours done? There's a very good woman in Auckland—I'll give you her name if you like—and she only costs eighty dollars or so.'

Bitch. She knew that Eden didn't have eight dollars to waste, let alone eighty. Eden gave her a cool smile. 'My mother always said this colour suited me, and so did Gran,' she replied serenely. Both had been extremely elegant women.

Jan gave a snide little laugh and shrugged. 'Oh, well,' she said, and concentrated the focus of her attention back to Blade. 'So you're going to be a permanent fixture on the scene. How nice for us all. I'm off to Fala'isi for the next few weeks, but you must come to dinner when I get back, and we'll introduce you to what passes as the social round in this neck of the woods.'

Blade lifted his brows, but said pleasantly, 'Thank you, I'd enjoy that.'

Jan turned her head sideways, gave Eden a particularly aggressive smile, and said on a sweet, false note, 'Oh, yes, of course, you too, Eden,' seeming not to notice the quick anger in Nick's expression.

Eden's first instinct had been to give a polite refusal, but Blade deserved the right to meet his neighbours socially, and if she said no he might refuse too. 'Thank you,' she said, deliberately remote.

Jan directed a spiteful glance at her, but she was enough in awe of her brother to behave reasonably well in his presence. 'It's about time you got out to see people,' she remarked. 'I'll give you a ring when I come back.' Her eyes lingered openly on Blade's face.

Without appearing to notice, he said smoothly, 'I'll look forward to that. And now we must go, I'm afraid.'

Nick said, 'So we can expect to see you at the next meeting, then?'

'Yes. Come on, Eden.' Blade smiled, a smile that didn't alter as he said goodbye to Jan, and stayed firmly in place as they walked towards the door. Then he said curtly, 'The next time you pull a stunt like that, I'll put you over my knee.'

Eden bit her lip, only too aware of the eyes following them as they moved out into the fierce glare of the sun. 'I didn't realise you were going to panic,' she replied stiffly. It hurt in some obscure fashion to be relegated to infant status. Put over his knee, indeed!

'I didn't know whether you had drowned or what the hell had happened.'

Eden looked up, and realised with alarm and dismay that he wasn't merely angry—he was furious. His eyes had darkened to stormy turbulence, and his mouth was a thin, straight line, ringed with white.

'I'm sorry,' she said huskily, touching his arm with a tentative gesture. Her hand jerked back, because to her overwrought imagination it seemed that once more the repressed energy inside him had been transferred electrically to her, shocking her with its intensity. The muscles beneath her fingers had been clenched hard, as unforgiving as the look he gave her.

'Try thinking occasionally,' he advised curtly. 'I know you've got into the habit of running wild, but if you and I are going to get on together I need to know that you're capable of behaving responsibly.'

The blatant unfairness of this had her saying hotly and childishly, 'I said I was sorry!'

'All right.' He took a deep breath, and she saw him reimpose his will over his emotions, bridle the anger with an ease that awed her.

By the car, he asked calmly, 'Do you want to go back to the beach?'

'I thought we were going home.'

'Did you want to stay there with them?' He watched her face closely as he finished, 'You're obviously very friendly with Stockley.'

She shrugged. 'I like Nick; he's been very kind to Grandad and to me, but I'm afraid Jan and I took an instant dislike to each other when we met fifteen years ago.'

'It showed,' he said brusquely. 'I doubt if she has much time for her own sex.'

Relieved that he was astute enough to see past Jan's dramatic, gypsy loveliness, Eden said lightly, 'Her loss. Why don't we go for a walk? I'm not a great one for sunbathing—I get hot and sticky and bored, and, even though I lather myself with sunblock, I tend to burn. But——'

Blade smiled without humour. 'I get bored, too. By all means let's walk. Where do you want to go?'

'Up to the golf course?'

It was a pleasant walk, although Eden couldn't control her emotions as easily as Blade was able to. And yet, she thought, eyeing him discreetly as they walked beneath the trees and watched the sun glint across the water, there was something not quite right about that calmness. He seemed to vibrate with a hidden energy, as though beneath the golden mask there were dangerous parts of him, parts he had to keep hidden and under restraint in case they got away.

They talked of the station, and he told her more of what he would like to do. Eden thought dreamily that she could spend the rest of her life doing this—walking with Blade, hearing his deep, deliberate voice, feeling a bubble of happiness expand until it irradiated the whole world for her, changing the beauty of the sea and the land to that of some faery country, unbearably exquisite, beyond understanding.

The only flaw in the day was the open interest in Blade that was evident in the eyes of many of the women they passed, intent and avid. What would it be like to be the recipient of such constant sexual speculation?

Eden wasn't beautiful; no man had gazed at her as though she was the sum of his desire. Just as well, she thought savagely, obscurely hurt. She wouldn't know what to do if any ever did!

But some small unregenerate part of her wondered what it would be like to have Blade look at her like that. Was that how he looked at the woman who rang him at least three times a week?

# CHAPTER FOUR

BACK at the yacht club, Eden sat down on the coarse grass and dusted the sand off her feet, her eyes fixed on to the bay. More yachts tacked to and fro, a whole fleet of small, brilliantly coloured sails.

'Do you know how to sail?' Blade asked, following the direction of her gaze.

'No. My mother would have had a fit if I'd even suggested it. Do you?'

'No. I grew up a long way from the sea. However, it's something I've always intended to have a go at, and this is the ideal place to learn. If sailing would have alarmed your mother, why do you ride a horse as though you were born on it?'

Eden flushed with pleasure. 'My mother didn't consider riding to be exercise, or exhausting,' she said, her smile inviting him to share the joke. 'For her it was a perfectly natural way to get from one place to the next, as normal as walking or running, and much more natural than swimming.'

'Was she phobic about the sea?'

'My father drowned.' It was the first time she had ever spoken about the tragedy to anyone but her mother and her grandmother.

Blade helped her to her feet, holding her hands in a gentle grip for a moment. 'I'm sorry,' he said quietly as he let her go.

She shrugged. 'He died before I was born, so I never knew him. He was a doctor; he went up to the Solomon Islands to help in a kind of medical safari, and he died one day while he was diving.'

'A great loss.'

77

'Yes,' she agreed a little wistfully. 'I wish I could remember him.'

'Do you know any of his relatives?'

She sent him a swift, oblique look. 'No,' she said shortly. 'He and my mother weren't married, and when he died his parents didn't want to know about her—or me. I think they were—very rigid in their views.'

'It happens,' he said, his face suddenly set in harsh angles. 'But it's their loss, not yours. Are you ready to go?'

'Yes.'

The trip back was hot, and, when they got on to their road, excessively dusty, made more so by the great cloud that rolled up behind a speeding ambulance as, with flashing alarm light, it hurtled around one of the corners towards them. Eden flinched.

'It's all right,' Blade reassured her, his hands relaxed on the wheel. 'He wasn't driving dangerously.'

'I know. It's just that—I went down to the hospital with Grandad. I've never liked ambulances since. I hope whoever it is is not too sick.'

When they arrived back she jumped out and ran inside, but her grandfather was sitting in the study talking to Mrs Clare, whom he knew well, as she was also the district nurse.

'Did you have a good swim?' he asked, smiling at them both as they came in through the door.

'Oh, it was lovely.' Eden beamed at Mrs Clare. 'Isn't it a magnificent day?'

'Wonderful.' Mrs Clare got to her feet, shrewd eyes surveying Blade. She smiled again, saying, 'I'm having a barbecue next Saturday, the first one of the season. We like to make a little party of it, and we ask most of our neighbours. We'd like it if you came too, Mr Hammond.'

'Blade,' he said, his smile sending curls of awareness through Eden. 'Yes, I'd enjoy that, thank you. It's time I learned who my neighbours are.'

She laughed. 'I believe you and Don have already talked over the boundary,' she said a little archly. 'We'll look forward to seeing you all, then, about five next Saturday.'

Eden watched with awe. If Blade's personal magnetism was so potent that Mrs Clare—a sensible, staid, happily-married matron—could actually flirt with him, then she need no longer feel so embarrassed by her own helpless response.

'Eden, the errant mail is actually yours,' Mrs Clare added. 'I'm afraid I read almost all of it before I realised it wasn't for me.'

'Postcards,' Eden said, accepting it, 'are fair game, I always think.'

It was from her godmother, Freda Chalfont. 'She's in Thailand,' Eden told them all. 'She says it's incredibly hot, and the people are exquisitely polite and don't sweat. The women are beautiful and have no hips. She has bought some silks.'

Sam grinned. 'That sounds like Freda.'

Mrs Chalfont, who definitely had hips, had been Linda Rogers' best friend all through boarding school and afterwards. Now widowed, with her adult children scattered around New Zealand and across the world, she had always kept closely in touch with Eden, staying quite often at Onemahutu. She had been Eden's saviour when Sam was ill, speeding up to help, so filled with calm confidence that Eden's panic had almost immediately subsided. Eden loved her dearly.

The week that followed was busy. Each day saw the men ride out on the station to deal with the repairs that were most urgent, working long hours. They left the homestead just after dawn and usually didn't come in, tired and dusty, until dusk. Once home, they ate the huge dinners Eden prepared for them, and then Paul went to bed while Blade spent much of his time either talking to Sam or working in the office.

Even when the repairs were done on Paul's house and he had moved into it, Eden continued to cook dinner for him, worried that he might not be bothered to do it for himself. Blade said nothing, so she concluded that he agreed with her reasoning.

Eden rebelled a little at being left in the house, but her grandfather was so pleased she was there to keep him company that she bit back her resentment. As December proceeded, the weather continued to be idyllic. Eden savoured it, relishing the intensifying warmth of the sun and the fresh green scents of the earth and the soft wind, the new growth.

The time she spent with Sam was made poignant by her knowledge that he might well not be with her this time the following year. Not that he dwelt on his frailty, or encouraged her to, either. With salty good humour he talked to her of her grandmother, and her mother, telling her old stories and incidents as though they were closer to him now than the present. Eden treasured every word, sometimes prompting him when he fell silent, sometimes learning something new. In those precious days she realised they were growing closer together than they had ever been. If for nothing else, she thought, she owed Blade for that.

Compelled by curiosity, she rode out on Rusty one afternoon when Mrs Clare was with her grandfather. She knew what the men had been doing on Onemahutu; each dinner they discussed it. But knowing was not the same as seeing.

As she looked around the evidence of their efforts were plain; the race had been re-metalled right back to the far boundary, and the worst fences were now standing upright, each post joined by tight wires that hummed softly in the breeze. It was quiet, the only sound the distant roar of a top-dressing plane as it spread its loads over Taunton Downs, the next station. As soon as it had finished there it would drop vital fertiliser on to

Onemahutu, and the grass would turn from its present faint yellow-green to a rich, lush emerald.

There was a faint breeze, just enough to carry a shrill whistle to her ears, and then barking. Eyes narrowed beneath the brim of her hat, Eden looked around, almost immediately picking up Abe's small figure on his horse in the puriri paddock. Two black and white dogs urged a mob of sheep through a gate.

Oh, but it was wonderful to see Onemahutu alive and active again!

They had drenched the lambs, and very soon they would be shearing, and she would be cooking for the massive appetites of the men who spent all day at that hardest of tasks. Unless of course Blade had decided to get in a gang that had its own cook, as they used to. She would have to ask him.

Daydreaming along, her mouth pulled into a soft reminiscent smile, she recalled how she used to sneak down to the wool-shed to watch Blade with the wondering eyes of hero-worship and the first stirrings of feminine need. She had been such a baby... Suddenly Rusty snorted, his head coming up as his ears twitched forward.

Sure enough, it was the men, working at the sheep-yards attached to the wool-shed, getting them ready for this year's shearing. Paul was hammering, while Blade lifted a length of timber and carried it with the smooth movements of great strength along to where another gap told of poor maintenance over the past years. Eden bit her lip, feeling as though it was her fault. Of course she was wrong; things had started to go wrong for her grandfather eight years ago, but sometimes logic wasn't able to convince.

When Rusty whickered both men looked up, instantly alert. She waved, and they responded, but went on with their work while she came down the hill towards them.

She was almost there when the top-dressing plane came roaring over the hill, its engine coughing. Spooked by the sudden, unexpected noise, Rusty pig-jumped, doing his best to dislodge her, so that it was a moment or two before she realised that the plane was making an irregular flight towards the Onemahutu air-strip, lurching in a peculiar pattern as though something was dreadfully wrong with it.

'Oh, God, please—no!' she whispered, her eyes straining into the sun as she followed its erratic flight. 'No!'

Her teeth clamped on to her lip. Pain seared through her lungs as she dragged in a shallow breath, and her stomach lurched with a hideous hollow thump, but she had flung herself to the ground, slung the bridle over Rusty's head, and was halfway to the Land Rover when the inevitable happened and there was a low, terrifying thud as the plane went into the ground behind a small hill.

The Land Rover was already going; Blade slowed enough for her to swing into it, and then they were heading across the paddock on a wild ride that had her clinging white-knuckled to the seat in front. Nobody spoke until they surged over the low crest of the hill and saw the plane, surprisingly intact. There was no sign of smoke or flame. Hope rose in Eden's heart.

'Stay there,' Blade snapped as he put on the brakes about four hundred metres away from the wreck.

Both he and Paul leapt out and raced across the grass, but as they neared it Blade shouted something and Paul stopped, reluctance plain in every line of his body.

'What is it?' Eden demanded, skidding to a halt beside him, but he didn't need to tell her. The stench of aviation fuel seared her nostrils. Horror suspended all rational thought; she knew now in a moment of stark, searing terror that if Blade died he would take her heart with him into the grave.

'No,' she croaked, watching as Blade wrenched open the door of the plane. 'Oh, God, if it goes up he'll be killed!'

She started forward, but Paul grabbed her wrist, his fingers painfully tight as he held her back. '*He'll* kill *me* if I let you go up there,' he said roughly, his eyes fixed on the plane and the man who was now half inside it. 'He told us both to stay put, and Blade's not a man to cross. He knows what he's doing.'

Eden flinched, but not even Paul could stop her when Blade dragged the pilot out and carried him in a fireman's lift down the hill.

'Get back!' he shouted as she came running towards him.

Eden hesitated, then turned back, grabbing for the first-aid kit she had noticed in the Land Rover. She had just wrenched it open when Blade arrived with his unconscious burden and set him down on the grass.

Eden knew what to do for the usual cuts and sprains that life on any farm made inevitable, but, as she knelt by the pilot and looked at his pale face, the features rendered indistinct by a mask of blood, she was afraid. However, she said sturdily, 'Where is he hurt?'

'One leg broken, at least, and head injury.' Blade's breathing had steadied. He must, she thought as she ran her hand along the pilot's legs, feeling for further breaks, be as strong as a bull. Only a man of superhuman strength could have carried a grown man so far.

'Possibly his back,' Blade added, the timbre of his voice altering.

Her hands froze. She lifted her head to look at his beloved face. It was carved in ice, all harsh angles. 'No!' she whispered.

He said savagely, 'I had to get him out. That bloody thing could have gone any minute—it could still go.'

'Of course you had to get him out.'

From the other side of the still figure on the ground, Paul said in a subdued voice, 'Bloody well risked yer life to do it. A man can't do more than that.'

Blade showed his teeth in a snarl. 'If his back is broken, he'll probably rather I'd left him there to die.'

'Nonsense! You had——' Eden broke off, realising that a car was bumping up the race towards them, travelling far too fast. 'Oh, thank heavens,' she muttered, hating the inadequacy that kept her from knowing what to do. 'It's Mrs Clare.'

Breathing easier, she gave way to the competent district nurse, who was followed half an hour later by a doctor. Then a helicopter arrived and took Blade and the doctor down to the base hospital at Whangarei.

Eden rode a nervous Rusty home, her expression sombre as she watched a fire engine, incongruous in its brilliant red against the peaceful pasture, spray foam over the crashed plane.

Three hours later, when Blade finally came back from the hospital, she and Paul were in the kitchen. He had just come in from milking the cow and she was preparing dinner. They heard the Land Rover come up the drive, and then nothing—no sound of footsteps, nothing.

Something cold clutched at Eden's heart. 'I wonder——?'

A door slammed. She started to take off her apron, but Paul said gruffly, 'Sometimes it's best to leave a man alone when he's got something on his mind.'

'And sometimes it's not,' she replied quietly.

Blade must have walked across the lawn to his room. He stood staring out of the window across the lawn and the bright gardens, his expression carved in granite. Eden knew that if she had any sense she'd turn around and leave him, but she came further into the room. He looked—lonely.

'What happened?' she asked quietly.

He didn't move. 'He died,' he said.

Her breath sighed out. Without thinking, wanting only to give what comfort she could, she slid her arms around his back, hugging him as hard as she could. 'You did everything you could to save him,' she soothed.

His chest lifted and fell. 'I killed him,' he said harshly.

Her arms dropped. She walked around to stand in front of him, looking sternly up into the chiselled stillness of his face. 'Don't be an idiot,' she told him sternly. 'If that plane had exploded he'd have died, and there was every reason to believe it was going up! I could smell the fuel from way back where I was. At least you gave him a chance. At considerable danger to yourself.'

He was watching her with cool, icy blue eyes, empty as a summer sky. 'He died of shock,' he said. 'His back was broken, but that needn't have been fatal. If he'd been taken out carefully——'

Eden reached up and shook his shoulders, but he was as immovable as a rock. 'And how would they have got him out?' she asked, the words tumbling out so fast that she was almost stammering. 'Cut him out? One spark and the plane would have gone up like an inferno. They'd have had to move him just to get him clear. You did what had to be done.'

'And killed him,' he said harshly, looking straight through her.

'Are you God, that everything should always go right for you? You did the only thing you could. You can't take the whole responsibility on your shoulders, Blade.'

Something moved in his eyes, something ugly, but at least he was looking at her, not into some bitter hell. 'How wonderful to have such a straightforward outlook,' he said softly. 'I did my best, so I'm exonerated from all blame. Just like that—so easy, so simple. But I have to live with myself.'

Her hands dropped to her side. She managed to stop herself taking a backward step, but it needed will-power. Instead, she stood her ground, saying softly, 'I'm sorry, Blade. Do you want me to go?'

A bleak, mirthless smile curled his beautiful mouth. 'No,' he said simply, and reached out to pull her into his arms, holding her crushed against him in a grip that rendered her completely breathless.

Bewildered, Eden had only just had time to work out that perhaps he needed the simple human comfort of a hug, when he tipped up her face and kissed her, long and slow, with a concentrated hunger that jolted through her like a bolt of lightning.

His mouth was warm and hard and sensuous, demanding everything from her. She shuddered, and then her heart jumped, for he lifted his mouth and said thickly, 'Open your mouth for me, Eden.'

Hot colour suffused her. She knew what sort of kiss he wanted, and, although she knew that it was considered extremely erotic, she wasn't sure that she wanted to kiss him like that.

And then it was too late, for he kissed her again, pulling her into him so that she could feel his hard body, rigid with the strain he had imposed on himself. She gasped, and he took his opportunity and probed deep inside. Eden's stomach bucked. Her pulses gained speed as he explored her mouth with shattering determination, kissing her as though she was infinitely precious to him, as though he wanted her more than he had ever wanted anything else in the world.

Drowning in sensation, her body ablaze, she willingly gave him what he asked for. He whispered something she couldn't hear above the erratic thunder of her heart, and lifted his mouth, but only to kiss the soft half-moons of her eyelids and the long arc of her throat. Each stinging little kiss sent her excitement soaring. Something untamed and primitive clutched at her with cruel claws, yet the implacable hunger was exquisitely pleasurable, melting through her like chocolate over warm toffee.

Eden was lost, unable even to lift her heavy lids, but she could smell him and taste him, and she was acutely aware of his body, lean and hard, against hers.

'Is this comfort you're offering,' he asked, his mouth coming to rest on the soft hollow at the base, 'or something else, Eden?'

The words didn't impinge. Until his hand slid up and cupped her breast.

That gentle touch branded her right through her skin to her bones, setting every cell and nerve-end on fire. Automatically she pulled away, her soft red mouth trembling with shock, her eyes dilated and dazedly green in her flushed face.

He wasn't smiling, as she had half thought he might be. With an impassive face, he surveyed her with insulting detachment, obviously not nearly as affected as she had been by those wild kisses.

Eden didn't know what to say, what to do. Humiliation dispatched the colour from her cheeks as she tugged down the hem of her T-shirt with trembling fingers. She turned away so that he couldn't see her clearly. Then, because it didn't seem as though he was going to say anything, she whispered, 'I don't think that's a good idea.'

'It was your idea,' he pointed out in a level, calm voice.

Flinching, she sought refuge in the mundane. 'I—I have to finish getting dinner.'

'Don't bother for me,' he said indifferently. 'I don't want any.'

'But——'

'Don't fuss.' The hurtful casualness seemed almost intentional. 'I'm not hungry.'

Eden left him, her mind as uneasy as her body, torn between offering him the comfort she sensed he needed, and the humiliating knowledge that she could not help him at all. Combined with the realisation that she had been absolutely no use at the scene of the crash, too, and the shock of the pilot's death, her emotions were a mixture that she couldn't even try to sort out.

She tried to push away the memory of those moments when she had lain against him, afire with unbidden desire, and given her whole heart into his keeping. Common sense told her that, while they had been the

most important moments of her life, they had not meant
nearly so much to him.

Blade didn't come to dinner. She didn't know where
he was, and if she went looking for him she feared
another rebuff, or, even worse, a repetition of that
heated, impersonal lovemaking.

'Leave him alone,' Paul advised again, not unkindly.
'He's a loner, deals with his problems in his own way.
He'll be all right.'

'Have you known him long?'

Paul gave a half-smile. 'Since he was a kid of eight
or so. Tough little beggar, even then—always big for his
age, and quiet, with too much self-control for a kid. I
remember when he was learning to ride a bike. He fell
off and tipped over and bloodied his knees, but he kept
going until he could ride it. Always took care of himself,
did Blade. And he never backed down from a fight—
didn't know how to.'

'He's taking it hard,' she said on a sigh.

'He's got feelings just like any other joker, but he keeps
them to himself. Always has. You never knew what he
was thinking, even when he was a kid. He'll be all right.
He's not the sort to buckle under, even if he does feel
it's his fault the bloke died. He's as tough with himself
as he is with others. He's the hardest man I know, harder
even than his father, and he was the toughest old bastard
I've ever come across.'

Abruptly, he stopped, eyeing Eden with an uneasy expression; then he shrugged. After a moment he finished,
'Don't worry about him. He won't thank you for it.
Never been one to ask for help, has Blade. He'll work
like a galley-slave until he's got rid of whatever's
worrying him, and then he'll be OK. He's not one for
feeling sorry for himself.'

So Eden sat up talking about the crash in subdued
tones with her grandfather until it was time for him to
go to bed, and then made her way to her own, her nerves
strung tight. It was all very well for Paul to say that

Blade was tough, but he was hurting, and it hurt her in some strange way that she couldn't ease his pain.

But she didn't dare go to him; he had taken her innocent offer of comfort as something else, and, although the memory of those kisses pulled her stomach tight with remembered excitement, Eden didn't want any more. She had been right to pull away, even though it had been like tearing off the other half of herself. He had not been kissing her—Eden Rogers. He had wanted to smother his pain in the maddened passion of making love, finding temporary solace in the most primitive rite of all.

She could not be content with that, she thought passionately; she wanted all of him—his whole life, his love. If she couldn't have that, she wanted nothing.

Much later, when every light had been out for ages, she wondered who his father was, the toughest man Paul had ever met. Perhaps that was why Blade didn't show his emotions; perhaps it had not been safe with such an unfeeling father.

He was remote the next morning, but more or less his normal self, for which Eden was devoutly thankful. The memory of those kisses was burnt into her brain, but, although his eyes seemed to linger on her periodically, she couldn't see beneath their burnished blueness to the emotions beneath. He ate his usual hearty breakfast.

'See, what did I tell ya?' Paul murmured before he followed Blade out to the Land Rover. 'He's right now.'

Was he? Or had Paul mistaken the reimposed control, that was so essential a part of Blade, for a quiet mind? His emotions ran very deep, she knew that now, and he kept them on a very tight leash indeed.

But surely, Eden surmised as she went about her work that day, he couldn't have kissed her like that if he hadn't felt something for her?

It was a thought she banished while dealing with the aftermath of the crash, referring reporters to the police, accepting calls from the inspector of air accidents, and from curious neighbours, then, in the middle of it all, having to tell the local policeman what had happened.

'Thanks,' he said when she'd finished. 'That has to be one of the bravest things I've heard of. Stupid, mind you. That plane was one tiny spark away from going up like a bomb. Don't know that I'd have gone anywhere near it.'

'I think Blade acted instinctively.'

He lifted his brows. 'When confronted by a crashed plane and the smell of aviation fuel, a man's instinct usually tells him to get the hell out of there,' he said. 'The man's got guts. Told me it had to be done, so he did it.'

That was what Blade would say. That kind of hard courage was one of the reasons Eden loved him. Because she knew now, had realised as she'd watched him run towards a plane likely to explode in flames at any second, that if he died she would never know this emotion again.

She was far too practical to hope for him to return her love. Men like Blade Hammond, formidably attractive, compelling and experienced, did not fall in love with gauche, nineteen-year-old girls. Even when he was kissing her she had known intuitively that there was no love for her in his embrace. But there was need, and hunger. A delicate wash of colour heated her skin. She might be a total innocent, but his body had been quite definite in its appreciation of her femininity.

That knowledge was like a secret pleasure, a hidden gift. She was sad for the pilot, appalled by the tragedy of his death and deeply sympathetic towards his grieving family, but deep inside she held those kisses like glowing talismans.

Blade worked too hard in the following days. Eden worried, but recalled Paul's summing up of his character, and assumed that he knew his employer and friend far better than she did. Blade would work his pain away.

On the Friday Mrs Clare came again, spending an hour with Sam before coming into the kitchen to gossip. She didn't say anything about the crash, for which Eden was devoutly thankful, but she did mention the barbecue.

Which had completely slid from Eden's mind.

'I did wonder,' Mrs Clare went on, 'whether we should put it off because of the crash, but, although it was tragic, none of us knew the man, and it's not as though he was a local.'

'No,' Eden said quietly.

'You and Blade went to his funeral, didn't you?'

Eden nodded. She had been torn between her sympathy for the dead man's family and being acutely aware of Blade beside her, wondering what he was thinking, how he was feeling. Afterwards, the pilot's widow had come across and thanked them for their efforts to save her husband. She had been very nice and clearly sincere, which had made it even more harrowing. Blade had been gentle and kind to her, but Eden had sensed turbulent emotions shielded behind the golden mask of his features.

She was sure he still blamed himself for the pilot's death; oh, probably not with the reasonable part of his brain. His cool male logic would accept the local policeman's view of his efforts—stupid, but brave. However, logic often had no defence against the more fundamental emotions. Blade believed that he had killed the pilot, and until he was able to deal with that he would put himself through a hell that he allowed no one else to share.

Eden had come close to thinking of him as a superman; she knew now that in spite of his air of confident command he had hidden vulnerabilities.

'So I'll expect you all about five tomorrow night.' Mrs Clare smiled. 'Everyone in the district is going to be there, all dead keen to meet the new owner of Onemahutu.'

That night when the new owner came in, uncommunicative and tired, Eden reminded him about the barbecue.

Judging by his expression, he had forgotten as well. Strong features rendered even more angular by tight control, he said something she just couldn't hear, then said curtly, 'All right, as we've accepted I suppose we'd better go, although I've felt more like socialising after a day's shearing. Is Nick Stockley likely to be there?'

Surprised, she shook her head. 'He's in Auckland.' He had called in to see Sam before he left.

Blade's eyes narrowed. 'Really? How do you know?'

When she told him he stood a moment, surveying her with a hooded gaze. Slow stirrings of excitement brought a faint tinge of dusky colour to her skin.

'How well do you know him?' he asked abruptly.

'Quite well. He comes to see Grandad quite often.'

'He has a bad reputation with women, I've heard.'

Eden's eyes flew to meet his, but she could see nothing but an oblique hardness. She said candidly, 'I've heard that too, but he's never been anything other than brotherly to me.'

Blade's eyes were frozen chips of ice. 'I should hope not,' he asserted acidly. 'You're only a baby.'

Which was about the most hurtful thing he could have said to her. Eden hoped she was able to hide the ache of humiliation his cruel words had given her, but she left him with the uneasy feeling that he had done it quite deliberately. Perhaps, she thought as she picked the last of the peas in the garden, he wanted to make sure she didn't get any ideas about those kisses.

A smile, half wry, completely humourless, lifted the corners of her mouth. Absently she slapped at a sandfly on her arm, and used her thumb to pod a row of gleaming green peas, popping the sweet morsels into her mouth as she blinked hard. She had no illusions about her attractions, none at all. He didn't have to hurt her by emphasising her lack of experience, how far away she was from him. She knew.

After lunch on the day of the barbecue Eden realised she had nothing to wear. A quick search of her wardrobe

revealed several pairs of jeans, far too faded and old to
wear out, a skirt she had worn three years ago, two sun-
dresses that looked rather the worse for wear, and several
outfits that she kept for town, including the water-
melon-coloured skirt and blouse she often wore to the
beach.

Eden pressed her lips together. The lawyer and the
accountant were finalising their affairs, but, until she
knew how they stood, she didn't dare spend anything
on clothes.

The Clares's barbecues were fairly casual, but the
women dressed for them in pretty clothes, make-up...
It had never worried her before, but now Eden wanted
to wear something as attractive and flattering as the other
women.

With her only lipstick in her hand, she sat down on
her bed and stared at the wardrobe, blinking back stupid
tears. A great wave of yearning for her mother and her
grandmother crashed her on to familiar shores of grief.
She wanted things to be the way they had been, when
her grandfather had been fit and well, and there had
been laughter and love in her life. She had done her best,
but the house had grown sad, and Onemahutu had gone
downhill, and now it didn't belong to them any longer.

'All this because you haven't got anything new and
pretty to wear to a barbecue!' she muttered scornfully,
getting to her feet. 'And because you are stupid enough
to love a man who sees you as a baby!'

After all, things were a lot better than they had been
only a month or so ago. As though her lack of clothes
mattered! Everyone knew her—but then, it wasn't the
neighbours she wanted to look good for.

In the end she decided on the most presentable pair
of jeans and the watermelon shirt, with the sandals she
had worn to the beach. She washed her hair, brushing
it until it shone, and slid into her ears the tiny gold hoops
her mother had bought for her tenth birthday. For long,
critical seconds she stared at herself in the mirror. Her

skin glowed with a faint, healthy sheen, green lights gleamed beneath the thick dark fans of her lashes, and the lipstick made her mouth look soft and full.

Perhaps tonight Blade would come out of that dark aloofness that had wrapped him like a cloak since the pilot's death, and—— She shivered, remembering those kisses, her mouth curving into a secret, seductive smile.

His voice outside her door made her jump. 'Are you ready?' he asked.

'Yes.' She felt oddly breathless, but she was still smiling when she went out.

He was wearing a casual shirt the pale, clear colour of his eyes, and a pair of darker trousers. He looked superb.

Her eyes shone as she smiled up at him. 'Grandad's ready too,' she said, trying to clamp down on the bubble of breathlessness. 'I'll go and get him.'

The Clare family lived on a smallholding, five acres of pasture and five of native bush, with a stony-bottomed creek running through the trees. A computer expert who worked from home, Mr Clare was an ardent gardener and landscaper, so the long, low house of stained weatherboards was in lovely surroundings. The barbecue area was a small dell in the bush, paved with old bricks, set about with azaleas and rhododendrons and other shade-loving plants. It was easy enough to get a car down there, so Sam didn't have to walk any distance. Eden was delighted to see how many of his friends were there, and how pleased they were to see him.

It was a strange evening. She knew most of the people there, of course, and introduced Blade to as many of them as she could, but it was soon obvious that she didn't need to worry about him. He might have grown up on a high-country station miles from anywhere, but he now possessed a sophisticated courtesy which, backed by his stunning masculinity, made him an asset to any social occasion.

She didn't like to presume on their acquaintanceship by sticking close to him, and, as Sam was busy talking with his old friends, and there were few people of her age there, she found herself eventually, after a quick round of greetings and conversation, helping Mrs Clare with the cooking.

'That colour suits you perfectly,' her hostess commented kindly.

Eden had to force herself to smile. Her hopeful anticipation of the evening had somehow sunk into ashes. 'Thank you. I love it,' she said cheerfully, turning sausages.

'Have you met the Blairs yet?'

Eden shook her head. 'No. They're the people who bought the Sampsons' place, aren't they?'

'Yes. A nice couple, with a very handsome son, about twenty-one or two.' She smiled. 'They'll be coming along soon. Tod saw you in town one day and was very curious about the pretty girl with the long brown hair and green eyes. When he heard you were going to be here he was delighted.'

A small warmth struggled into being in Eden's heart. It was nice to be admired. She glanced across at Blade, watching with something like pain as he smiled down at a very attractive woman, the unmarried daughter of one of the neighbours, and felt the glow extinguish, just like that. Flaring torches cast their reddish glow on his face, boldly picking out the autocratic outline, the superb bone-structure, the crease of cheek as he gave a purely male smile.

From the way the woman was looking at him, Eden thought disdainfully, she had never seen anyone so fascinating in her life. With an effort she wrenched her eyes back to the job in hand, fighting down an enormous and sudden desolation.

'Ah, there are the Blairs,' Mrs Clare said happily. 'Come and meet them, Eden. Those sausages aren't going to burn if we leave them for a while.'

Tod Blair was attractive, with bold brown eyes and a brash smile, and there was no mistaking the appreciation in both eyes and smile when he met Eden.

However, instinct warned her that there was something a little insolent in his attitude, and although she talked pleasantly to him she was cautious, refusing to respond to his overt flirtation with anything more than a quiet friendliness. Compared to Blade's quiet strength, Tod's confidence was too presumptuous.

Eden didn't notice the hard spark of anger in the younger man's eyes when she refused to respond to his gallantry, nor would she have cared overmuch if she had.

But she soon realised that he seemed determined to attract her attention, making for her whenever he could, so that over the next few hours she developed a slight hunted feeling. Not that he said anything she could object to. He was fun, and she would have been abnormal not to be mildly flattered by his obvious interest, but apart from common courtesy she had nothing to give him. And he stood too close.

It almost seemed as though her guarded response, her reserve, spurred his interest. There was another girl there, a year younger than Eden and much prettier, who spent most of the evening casting him sideways looks through flirtatious lashes, but he ignored her.

All in all, Eden was glad when she saw her grandfather look about for her. The circles under his eyes had darkened and the hand that grasped his stick trembled slightly, so it was more than time that she took him home.

'I'm afraid I have to go; Grandad's tired,' she said, stepping back once more.

Tod's face fell. 'So early?' he asked incredulously.

'Yes.'

But he followed her across, asking, 'Can I see you again? Look, I'll give you a ring, shall I, and we can go out together one night?'

She hesitated, and he said smoothly, 'Just to the pictures, perhaps?'

'I don't think so,' she said gently. 'My grandfather needs me.'

'I'll give you a ring,' he stated confidently.

Something in his tone warned Eden that Tod Blair was not a man who was turned down often, but she was relieved that he had offered her an easy way out; she could always say no over the telephone.

Blade must have been keeping an eye on them, for he appeared almost immediately, silently, like a great golden cat. 'Ready to go?' he asked smoothly, smiling at Tod, who looked a bit taken aback.

Eden cast him a grateful glance. 'Yes. Grandad is looking a bit weary.'

'I'll get him. See you at the car.'

'Who's he?' Tod asked a little belligerently, his eyes lingering on Blade's tall figure as he made his way across to Sam.

'He bought our property from us.'

Tod swivelled his glance back to her. 'So?'

'We haven't moved out yet.' She gave him a sweet, deliberately vague smile, and said, 'I must go. Goodnight.'

But he insisted on coming across to the car with them, and she felt again that faint feather of unease as he bent and said softly, 'Goodnight, Eden. I'll catch you later.'

Tired though he was, it was obvious that Sam had enjoyed the evening immensely. He chatted with Blade all the way home, and Eden sat in the back of the car, wondering why she was so exhausted. Jealousy, she supposed. It had been as if a horrible black cloud had descended on her when she'd seen Blade smile at that woman. She had hated the bitter, dragging emotion, but had been unable to banish it, even though she had no right to be jealous.

Perhaps, she thought sardonically, she had been spoilt, being the adored only child and grandchild. She was going to have to curb her inclination towards possessiveness. Apart from any other woman, there was Thea.

Going by the sound of Blade's voice when he spoke to her, he liked her very much. It was impossible to tell exactly what relationship they shared; Eden took good care not to listen, and Blade didn't give anything away.

After she had taken Sam his cup of beef tea, she asked Blade, who was standing out on the veranda, whether he wanted something to drink.

'No, thank you.' His voice was as remote as the stars that shone around the outline of his head.

'Right, goodn—— What's that?'

But even as she said the word she knew what it was. A meteor spun halfway across the sky before burning up into darkness in the earth's atmosphere. Of itself, that was not so unusual, but it was almost immediately followed by another, and then another and another, all coming from one particular area of the sky.

'A shower of them!' Blade exclaimed, something of the primeval awe of the unknown reflected in his deep voice.

'I saw the aurora once.' Eden leaned out over the balustrade to see better. The scent of datura was sweetly evocative on the cool air. 'It was like a green curtain in the sky. We don't have it very often up here, so far from the South Pole.' Sly humour danced in her voice. 'I suppose you grew up with it as a night-light. But I've never seen anything like this—oh, look, four or five of them all at once!'

'Heavenly fireworks,' he said drily. 'And no, we didn't see much of the aurora either, although probably more than you. The South Island isn't exactly Antarctica, you know.'

Another shower of eight or nine meteors stopped her riposte before the words left her mouth. Silently, they watched the amazing display until at last it faded and died, leaving the heavens as remote as they usually were, the stars moving slowly in their immutable paths.

'That was wonderful,' she declared softly. It was cool and clear, and the crisp air made her shiver.

'You'd better get inside.'

Eden didn't want to go; she wanted to stay out there with him. But he was right; she was getting cold. 'Goodnight,' she said reluctantly.

'Goodnight.' His voice was very deep, very soft, as though he had been as affected by the meteor shower as she had.

It did strange things to the pit of her stomach. So strange that she tripped as she was going through the french window, and might even have fallen if he hadn't caught her. Her breath stopped in her throat. For one glorious moment she felt his strong hands on her shoulders, and then he put her back on her feet and said curtly, 'Look where you're going.'

Eden was still smiling as she took off her watermelon blouse and the jeans. Although his voice had been curt and harsh, she had felt his hands tremble, and some deeply womanly part of her knew that he had wanted her at that moment.

She dreamed all night, delicious dreams of making love with him in the big kauri bed, of being kissed by him, of living with him in some cloudland of romance... dreams when his voice thickened sensuously as he told her that he loved her, he couldn't live without her, that Thea had just been a temporary aberration...

No wonder she woke heavy-eyed and exhausted. It was just as well Blade and Paul and Abe took packed lunches and morning and afternoon teas, and worked all day on the back-boundary fence, because she was sure that her hopes and fantasies were still imprinted on her face, lurking at the back of her eyes for anyone to decipher.

Her grandfather was tired, but, although he spent much of the day dozing off in his chair, he didn't look any the worse for his late night. Eden watched him, loving him with all her heart. It was another thing to thank Blade for—the renewal he had given Sam, the freedom from worry and the constant irritation of knowing that his granddaughter was working far too hard because he was no longer able to do anything.

That evening she cooked a superb meal, starting with fresh asparagus from the garden served with butter, followed by lamb noisettes with basil and a blackcurrant sauce that had been her mother's favourite. Eden had scrubbed tiny new potatoes, also from the garden, and for pudding she had made a fresh fruit salad of tangelos and kiwi fruit and bananas, served with cream.

'You're as good a cook as your grandmother,' Sam told her when he had finished.

Eden smiled. 'I should be; she taught me how to cook!'

Both were silent a moment, then Sam said, 'I think I'll be turning in.'

# CHAPTER FIVE

BLADE waited until Sam had gone before asking quietly, 'When did your grandmother die?'

'Four years ago.' She began to gather the dishes together, not looking at him. 'Six weeks after my mother died of cancer. It was the year after you came,' she finished inanely. Her mouth trembled.

'I was in Australia then.' He picked up the bowl that had held the fruit salad and went with her out into the kitchen.

'When did you come back?'

His face hardened. 'I had to come back two years ago. I've been working in the South Island since then.'

Eden said swiftly, 'I'm glad it was you who bought Onemahutu. Grandad hasn't looked so well since he had the stroke. It means a lot to him to be able to see it come back to life.'

He must have divined what she was thinking, for he said, 'You did your best, Eden, and that's all anyone can do. You survived.'

Pouring detergent into the battered, reliable old dishwasher, she closed the door then set the cycle. 'Sometimes I hated Onemahutu,' she revealed, not looking at him, speaking with difficulty at first as the words tumbled out, awful words, telling him things she had never admitted even to herself. 'I began to think that I was going to spend the rest of my life working myself to death on it for no result, just seeing it all go backwards and never being able to catch up.'

She darted a glance at him, searching for disgust, but he said, 'I don't blame you. It must have felt like a fetter around your throat.'

101

She gulped, and the words came more freely, hoarse with frustrated emotion. 'It became almost a person, a great, greedy monster sucking my life away before I'd had a chance to live. I felt as though it had killed my mother and my grandmother, and crippled Grandad, and that it was going to kill me. I was desperate to get off it, to see the world, to do something that——' Horrified, she closed her eyes.

Blade looped an arm around her shoulders, hugging her close to the sanctuary of his big body, warm, amazingly comforting. 'Go on,' he said calmly.

Eden drew a deep, trembling breath. 'I felt as though it was a prison,' she continued in a small voice. 'Sometimes I thought I was never going to be free of it, never going to be able to do what I wanted to do, to—to experience new things, to play, and travel, and see what the world is like. To be *young*. I was going to university, but I couldn't leave Grandad...' She gulped. 'I sound so selfish,' she finished on a shuddering sigh.

'No.' His voice was kind, yet abstracted, as though he was barely paying attention to her. 'You poor little scrap; you've had a hell of a time, haven't you?'

She bit her lip, afraid that he was despising her selfishness. His arm tightened about her.

'You have a right to your dreams,' he said slowly. 'You've been working too hard, too long, with no hope and precious little thanks. It was far too much for you, but at least you tried, Eden. You did what you had to, without whining or giving up. You can pride yourself on that, now it's all over.'

Eden leaned her head against his chest, her eyes closing, her emotions a complete turmoil. She could smell him, that faint yet immeasurably potent scent of masculinity, erotic, exciting. He smelt of—man. Her man.

Thrilled by his nearness, she lifted her face, unconsciously seeking his kiss, her lashes lifting to reveal eyes green and smoky with desire. His face hardened; even as she realised how she must look, shamelessly offering herself, he loosened his arm and stepped away, the mask crashing down to hide his thoughts.

'I'd better get into the office and do some work,' he said tonelessly, and walked out.

Shame bit into her with its keen edge, smearing a murky film over her thoughts and emotions. Her skin heated as colour rushed through it. Blade couldn't have made it more obvious that, whatever he had wanted, it was not to kiss her. He had made a gesture of comfort, and she had misconstrued it, and made a fool of herself.

First of all she'd poured out an almost hysterical diatribe, and then she'd made things infinitely worse by giving off signals like a traffic-light, until he had been forced to walk away. So much for those romantic, forbidden dreams of the night before!

While the water sloshed around the dishwasher she stayed hidden in the kitchen, lashing herself with bitter recriminations, but slowly she realised that she wasn't going to get anywhere by cowering away. The only way she could salvage some pride was to treat Blade with a throw-away friendliness, as though absolutely nothing untoward had happened.

So she greeted him the next morning with a smile, and eyes that were as open and guileless as she could make them, withstanding his narrowed stare with hard-won fortitude.

It seemed to work, and, although her heart ached, she kept it up, buoyed by a still cold pride that she hadn't known she possessed.

The following evening Blade answered the telephone, then said in his most unemotional voice, 'It's for you, Eden.'

'Hello,' she said cautiously.

'Eden? It's Tod Blair here. How would you like to come to the pictures with me tomorrow night? It's a really good one—Meryl Streep.'

'Oh——' She set her mouth and told him firmly, 'Yes, I'd love to, thank you.'

'Good.' He sounded pleased but not surprised, not nearly as surprised as Eden was now that she had accepted. 'I'll pick you up around seven-thirty.'

'Yes, that will be fine.'

Perhaps by going out with another man she might be able to dull the ache that had become so much a part of her.

'Who was that?' Blade asked casually.

'Tod Blair.'

He lifted his brows. She met that faintly inimical look steadily, refusing to capitulate. A wry smile tucked in the corner of his mouth. 'Don't look so defiant,' he said softly, deflating her. 'I don't mind if you go out with him.'

But her grandfather asked testily, 'Who is this boy? Who are his family? Do we know them?'

Conscious of Blade's amusement, Eden said shortly, 'You met them at the Clares' barbecue, remember? They've bought the Sampsons' place.'

'Ah, yes, I remember. Didn't like the boy much— decent enough manners, but a bit brash.'

She kissed his brow. 'Grandad, you think anyone under sixty is a bit brash!'

He grinned, but warned, 'I want to meet him before you go; make sure you bring him in.'

'Yes, of course I will!'

She wore her watermelon shirt and skirt, hoping that Tod Blair was like most men, in never remembering what women wore, and, with an oddly self-possessed attitude for what was her very first outing with a man, waited for him on an evening that was warm and cloudy, with the smell of rain in the air. One thing about being violently attracted to one man, she thought cynically, was that it made you very calm when going out with others. She wasn't racked by anxiety or diffidence.

Blade's silent arrival made her look up. He said, 'Where are you going?'

'To the pictures in town.'

He nodded, and sat down opposite her, his expression a little abstracted. Perhaps something was worrying him, she thought with her usual astuteness where he was concerned.

But he asked absently, 'How many men have you been out with?'

Flakes of rose outlined her cheekbones. She replied shortly, 'None.'

He sighed. 'Did you and your mother discuss——?'

'I know the facts of life,' she interpolated, horribly embarrassed.

'It would be hard to live on a farm and not,' he said tonelessly. 'However, it isn't the facts of life I'm thinking of, exactly. More the spring, and a young man's fancy, and exactly what he's likely to construe love as.'

Green shimmered beneath her lashes as she composed her expression into demureness. He didn't look embarrassed; he looked as though he had been counselling young virgins on their first date all his life. Just once, she thought with a touch of acid, she would like to see him with that massive self-control punctured. Just once.

'And exactly what is he likely to construe love as?' she asked solemnly.

'Sex.'

A great wash of colour flooded Eden's throat and face. She hadn't expected such bluntness, and she didn't know how to respond. Fortunately Blade didn't seem to expect her to say anything, for he leaned back in his chair, regarded the long stretch of his legs thoughtfully, and went on, 'In fact, that's what most men think about all the time. So, if you don't want him to feel that he's struck lucky, make it obvious that you are, in the terminology of our mothers, a "good girl".'

'And how do I do that?'

He lifted his lashes, catching the last of her blush. His eyes were unfathomable, like blue quartz. 'Don't allow him familiarities you're not comfortable with,' he said, his voice even and dispassionate. 'If he wants to park, it will be for one reason only. And what your mother said is quite correct: if you set a value on yourself, your company and your body, then men will value you accordingly.'

Did Blade no longer respect her because she had let him kiss her, and asked—no, begged—for it to happen again? Or did he think she was such an innocent that he had to tell her all this so that she wouldn't do the same with someone else, and be treated with contempt?

She didn't know, and she was embarrassed and a little angry with him. But she held her head high, and said, 'Thank you,' with as much dignity as she could produce.

'Did your mother tell you how to disable a man, if you feel the need?' he asked.

Her eyes widened. 'No. Do you mean self-defence techniques?'

'Exactly.' He told her simply and graphically exactly how to incapacitate any man who attacked her, viewing her blushes with something like anger. 'Every woman should know how to look after herself,' he finished crisply. 'And remember, too, that you can say no whenever you want to, and expect the man to stop. Immediately, although probably not without ardent attempts to persuade you that they can't.'

She blushed again, grateful yet a little piqued that he could be so clinical. 'Thank you,' she said again.

His smile was edged with irony. 'I would rather have liked a sister,' he observed.

So that was how he thought of her. It hurt, but she held her head high. Instead she murmured politely, 'You are very kind.'

His mouth twisted. 'Always to you,' he startled her by saying. 'Is that a car? I'll let him in.'

Which he did, ushering Tod into the room where she had taken refuge with her grandfather. She was glad to see that Tod treated the older man with a deferential courtesy that satisfied her grandfather, but it amused and surprised her when he spoke to Blade the same way.

It was a pleasant evening. She enjoyed the film, and afterwards he brought her straight back home, talking a little about the film, but infinitely more about Tod Blair. At the door, she said, 'Would you like to come in for a cup of coffee?' and he said that, yes, he would very much.

The house was dark except for a single light from Blade's bedroom that indicated he was still awake. Eden led the way into the kitchen and put the kettle on, reaching up to pull cups and saucers down from the cupboard.

She turned her head to say something, and saw that Tod was watching the way the material of her blouse stretched over her slight breasts. He was smiling, but there was no humour in his expression, only a predatory alertness that sent a slight shudder to tighten her skin. He wasn't licking his lips, but that was what he reminded her of—a big animal seeing something that it wanted and was determined to have. She felt smirched, rendered unclean by the eager light in his eyes.

So this was what Blade had meant when he said all young men had their minds on sex!

'Milk and sugar?' she asked, making her voice crisp to cover her uneasiness.

'Just milk,' he said a little thickly.

But he had stopped watching her in that intent way, and the smile on his lips was genuine, albeit a little lazy and self-satisfied. After a while her distaste faded; she decided with taut humour that he couldn't help it if his hormones were surging, and he had been good company.

They drank the coffee in the little parlour, and then she went out to the front door with him, walking down the path between rows of night-scented stocks to the gate.

There, he turned and slid his arms around her, and, with an expertise that spoke of considerable experience, kissed her, softly at first, then with the same thrust of his tongue that had so startled her when Blade had done it.

She stiffened, turning her head away, and he let her go, his eyes gleaming in the starlight. 'Goodnight,' he said a little roughly. 'I'll ring you tomorrow.'

Eden hesitated, not knowing whether she wanted him to contact her again, but he was already swinging down to his car.

After he had gone she walked slowly back up to the house, trying to work out what had happened. He had kissed her. She had enjoyed the first kiss, but the second had made her stomach turn. Yet when Blade had kissed her like that, she had lost herself in it.

She sighed, wondering why she had to fall in love with a man who was so much older, so far out of reach. The agony of despair and pain that she had been keeping under control threatened to burst loose, but she fought a bitter, silent battle, and kept it leashed.

'Why the heavy sigh?'

The amused question made her jump. 'Where are you?' she demanded, whirling around.

Blade had been under the magnolia, leaning against the trunk, but as she spoke he came out into the starlight, moving with the lithe grace of a panther, sleek and powerful, almost threatening in the sweet scents of the Victorian garden. 'Sorry,' he said, not sounding in the least like it, 'did I frighten you?'

'You did, a bit.' She was awkward, ill-at-ease, and resentful. She was not so childish that she needed someone—even the man she rather suspected she loved— to wait up for her. And she cringed at the thought that he might have witnessed those kisses.

'Now why,' he mused, stopping a few feet away, 'why do I get the idea that you weren't in the least frightened?'

'Startled is probably a better word,' she agreed, recovering her composure. 'What were you doing, lurking under the tree?'

He smiled. 'I needed fresh air,' he said obliquely. 'How was the film?'

'Good. Marvellous in fact. But then, Meryl Streep always is.'

He had seen the film, and for a few minutes they discussed it. Eden had been a little frustrated when talking it over with Tod, who had said that he'd liked it, but didn't seem to know why. Blade was able to discuss his reactions intelligently and provocatively.

But then, she thought, Blade was a man, and Tod was only a grown-up boy!

And she shivered, racked again by some primeval pain.

'Let's go inside,' he said immediately.

It was sweetly painful to walk up the path beside him, to go in through the door that he held open, to turn in the dimly lit passage and say goodnight. He smiled, but behind the conventional gesture was the constraint that had been a barrier between them from the first.

He was so unyielding, so intensely shielded by the golden mask of his features. It was impossible to tell what thoughts were quickening in that shrewd, determined brain. In spite of her close surveillance she had no idea whether he was in love with Thea, or whether the woman was merely his mistress—someone with whom he had an arrangement that satisfied them both but didn't touch his heart.

So how, she asked herself despairingly as she got into bed, how could she love him? Surely you had to know someone to love him? She knew more about Tod Blair than she did of Blade. But then, Tod wasn't at all averse to talking about himself.

Was she just physically attracted to Blade? She was nineteen—old enough to mate, to have children; had she seen him as the most potent man available, and chosen him for that reason?

No, she thought with swift revulsion. That would make it merely physical, and, although her body registered his presence in a thousand delicate ways, she loved him for much more than the way he made her feel. She admired him for his determination, and respected his intelligence, she was warmed by his kindness, and if her heart performed strange flips when he smiled at her with narrowed eyes, that was more than matched by the pleasure she got from talking to him, matching wits with him, discussing ideas and projects and affairs with him. He was strong, mentally as well as physically. And he was compassionate as well as kind.

But when she tried to probe delicately beneath the surface, to make a tentative map of his emotions, she came up against the gleaming mask, the polished sophistication that reflected back only what he wanted her to see.

Whereas she was young, and naïve, and totally lacking in any kind of worldliness. He must, she thought bitterly, recalling that oddly tender little talk he had given her on the habits of young men, think of her as the original innocent.

Just for a moment, a weak, tentative moment, she allowed herself to dream... Of life as his wife here at Onemahutu, of days spent in its green bowl of hills, hardworking, satisfying. Of nights spent in his arms in the big kauri bed, impassioned nights that she could only imagine... Of children growing up on the station— laughing children, a daughter like her father, a son like his mother...

Closing eyes that were suddenly hot and aching, Eden pushed her face into the pillow. It would never happen; it was just fantasy, beguiling, dangerous. And she was going to have to stop it as long as she lived here. She would have to pretend that she felt nothing more for Blade than a sisterly affection, and when it was time she would leave and never come back again.

Because she had nothing to offer a man like Blade, nothing except this primal call in the blood, the instinctive, cell-deep knowledge that they would be good together in the most primitive ritual of all—the mating rite.

He needed so much more. He needed a woman with the same sort of deliberate discipline, someone with restraint and dignity and sophistication. Because Blade was not going to be just a station-owner for the rest of his life. At the Clares' barbecue Eden had noticed several of the men talking to him about the politics of farming, sounding him out. Like Nick Stockley, they had recognised his effortless authority. Of course Blade would become involved in the public, executive side of farming as well. And he would need a wife who could hold her own in any sort of company. Not a girl who hadn't even gone to school, who had no friends, no contacts, not a scrap of sophistication at all!

She woke the next morning with a slight headache, although it dissipated soon after she got up. Over breakfast her grandfather demanded to know all about the outing the evening before, so she told him, aware that Blade was silently listening.

'What time did you get home?' Sam asked casually.

'Eleven o'clock.' Eden sent him a teasing smile. 'I gave him a cup of coffee then sent him on his way.'

Sam grinned back. 'Just as well. I may be old, but the shotgun is still in good order.'

She gave him a haughty look. 'Don't start scrubbing it,' she said pertly as she poured him another cup of tea.

'You don't scrub shotguns, girl! I thought I'd taught you better than that!'

It was like old times, this teasing, and she had the silent man on the other side of the table to thank for it. Until Blade had arrived, like an extraordinarily handsome angel, Sam had fast been sinking into gloom.

Overcome by some gratitude and delight, she smiled at Blade. Something darkened his eyes, and his answering smile was a little cool.

'Another cup?' she asked.

'No, thanks, I'd better be on my way.' He got to his feet, effortlessly dominating the room, said, 'I'll see you at lunchtime,' and left, leaving the room empty and the atmosphere flat.

Eden bit her lip. Was she being absurdly sensitive to read some sort of rejection into those few words? And yet she was sure he had cut her off as clearly and definitely as though he had said the words.

Adjuring herself to stop being so stupid, she sat down to drink another cup of tea.

Tod rang again that night, suggesting that they go to a party at a friend's house that Saturday. 'Yes, that sounds fun,' Eden told him.

If he had shown any signs of falling in love she would have refused to go out with him, but she was certain that although he enjoyed her company he didn't feel anything stronger than a mild liking. And a soupçon of lust, she thought with a faint shudder, remembering that look.

'Right, I'll pick you up around eight,' he said with satisfaction.

'Who was that?' Blade looked up as she came into the room.

Eden replied a little distantly, 'Tod. We're going to a party at the Harveys' on Saturday.'

He lifted his brows, transfixing her with a cool, speculative stare. 'Did I meet any Harveys at the Clares' barbecue?'

She wanted to wriggle her shoulders to ease the tension between them, tension that had sprung up from nowhere. 'No, I don't think any of them were there,' she said, pretending to give the question her whole attention. 'They live about ten miles away, up at the end of Harvey's Road, on the right as you're going into town.'

'Got a big sheep and cattle stud,' Sam informed him. 'Angus and Romneys. Pohuihui.'

'No, I don't know them.' Blade looked down at his book again, but Eden was left with a niggling sense of disquiet. Probably because she was so attuned to him, she thought dismally, as she tried to work out what on earth she could wear to this party.

What did one wear to parties as distinct from barbecues?

In the end she chose slim black trousers she'd had since she was fifteen, and wore over them one of her mother's blouses—a pretty, airy thing of draped peach chiffon, setting off the outfit with black ballet slippers that had lurked in her wardrobe since she had given up ballet at thirteen. Fortunately her feet hadn't grown since then. She had on no make-up apart from lipstick, but, when she went into the study to wait, her stomach churning in anticipation, Sam looked up and said, 'You look pretty, m'dear.'

She smiled and kissed him, but the one man she wanted to notice her merely lifted his brows and gave a dry, wholly unimpressed smile. Not that she could blame him. No doubt Thea wore superb clothes with a model's panache. Compared to her, Eden thought dismally, aware that she was making unfounded assumptions, she probably looked like one of the little white peaches that ripened before Christmas against the luscious Golden Queens in March. Immature, and not particularly tasty.

But as they heard the car drive up Blade came out with her into the hall and said, 'Remember, if young Blair drinks too much, give me a call and I'll come and get you.'

Astonishment lifted her gaze, but his face showed nothing but uncompromising authority, and his eyes were burnished enamel, brilliantly opaque. 'Yes, all right,' she agreed slowly.

'Enjoy yourself.'

She produced a smile. 'I have every intention of doing just that!'

She expected him to go, but he stayed beside her, greeted a smart Tod with his normal formidable courtesy, and finished by saying, 'I'll see you later, then. What time do you plan to be home?'

Embarrassment stopped the words in her mouth. Tod looked a little taken aback, but recovered swiftly to say, 'About one, or two, I'd say. Depends on how good the party is.'

'Make it one-thirty.' There was a note in the cool voice that warned them this was not negotiable.

'OK,' Tod said cheerfully, waiting until they were outside before asking curiously, 'What's with the body-guard bit?'

'Oh, he's that sort of man,' she returned airily, secretly wondering why Blade had put a time limit on her evening. She was angry with his heavy-handedness, but instinct warned her not to let Tod realise that. 'Responsible. I'll bet he'll be really tough on any daughters he has,' she finished, with enough of a lilt in her voice to defuse the moment.

He grinned. 'I wouldn't take the bet,' he said.

Eden was a little alarmed, on going into their big, sprawling house, to discover that the Harvey parents were not there, and that there were few people she knew among the guests. Neither were they greeted by Mark Harvey; instead, several people she had never seen before, whose names were unfamiliar, hailed Tod with every appearance of pleasure. He introduced them, and they stayed for a while chatting about nothing much until someone somewhere put on a tape to dance to.

'Catch you later,' Tod finally said, grinning. He took Eden's hand in his, and led her to a big room at the back of the house which had clearly been set up for entertaining.

Eden was pleased to see that her outfit was perfectly all right; in fact, she thought, eyeing the other women there, she could have turned up in anything, including her nightgown, and it would have been acceptable.

The party was not exactly what she had expected. People seemed to come and go, and the noise level was incredible, with music throbbing so loudly that it was almost impossible to conduct any sort of conversation.

Fortunately Tod enjoyed dancing, so they spent most of their time among the ever-changing crowd in the entertainment room.

Occasionally they stopped for a drink, but after Eden had drunk half of a glass of orange juice she realised that someone had added alcohol to it, so she refused any more.

The evening was a little bewildering; mostly the men seemed to know each other, and the women, who were her age or younger, stayed close beside whoever had brought them. Even in the rooms where there was no dancing, there seemed to be little conversation; on a trip to the bathroom she passed by a couple of rooms where there was a lot of shouting and laughing going on, in an uncontrolled way that alarmed her a little.

Halfway back she was accosted by a man who leaned against the wall, imprisoning her, and said with a leer, 'And who are you, pretty girl? I don't know you, do I?'

His speech was a little slurred, Eden noticed with distaste.

'No,' she said calmly, and ducked under his arm, her heart hammering in her chest. Another great burst of laughter came from one of the rooms. A little further along she came upon a couple embracing, the man's hand groping up beneath the woman's clinging blouse to caress her back in a manner Eden thought too intimate for such a public place.

It was turning into the sort of party she definitely didn't want to be at. Back in the room she looked around for Tod, and saw him talking to another couple. He laughed, then lifted a small bottle of beer to his mouth and drained it all. He was flushed, but when she rejoined them he seemed perfectly all right, with no suspicious slurring of his words, no lurching step.

As she came up to him the music started again, a little softer and definitely more slow than before. Tod grinned at the two he had been talking to, and pulled Eden back on to the floor. He was an excellent dancer, although he held her just too close. 'Enjoying yourself?' he asked in her ear.

She bit her lip, looking around the room. Everything suddenly seemed tawdry; as she watched, another couple embraced passionately in the corner. She felt slightly sick.

'Yes, it's been fun so far,' she said. 'But I'm not used to all this noise; I think I'm getting a headache.'

He lifted his brows, his eyes narrowing, then cast a quick glance at his watch. 'Poor thing,' he said sympathetically. 'Let's go, then.'

No one said goodbye, no one even seemed to notice that they were going. Even as they went down the drive, a pair of headlights swung off the road and came towards them.

'Looks set to go all night,' Tod commented, pulling over into a gateway.

'Did you want to stay longer?'

He chuckled. 'No way.'

'I didn't see Mark Harvey at all,' Eden remarked in a surprised tone as the oncoming car swept past them to the accompaniment of tooting and a few yells.

'He was around,' Tod returned casually. 'Enjoy yourself?'

'Yes,' she said with a polite lack of truth, leaning her pounding head back against the seat. It hadn't developed into a full-blown headache, thank heavens, but much more of that noise and she'd have had to take something for it. As it was, the throbbing was already starting to ease.

Tod drove slowly and carefully along the road. After a moment Eden relaxed and closed her eyes, falling into a slight doze. When the car stopped she sat up again, ready to thank him and go inside. But, instead of the homestead, they appeared to be in a leafy grotto, surrounded by long, drifting fronds of weeping willow. The council metal-dump, she realised after a startled moment.

'Nobody can see us here,' Tod said with satisfaction, unclipping his seatbelt. 'We're way off the road.' His hand reached for her clip, and as she struggled to work out what was happening he said casually, 'Let's get into the back; there's not enough room to manoeuvre here.'

'I don't want to manoeuvre!' she blurted, trying to keep her voice light as Blade's warnings leaped into her mind.

A sudden coarse note invaded his voice. 'Come on, Eden, you don't have to be coy; I knew what you had in mind when you suggested we leave early. We've got at least three-quarters of an hour——'

'I'm sorry,' she cut in firmly, feeling a complete idiot. 'I wanted to come home early because I've got a headache. I—I gave you the wrong impression——'

She could smell the alcohol on his breath and, with a catch in the rhythm of her heart, wondered just how much he'd had to drink.

'So you're a tease,' he said thickly, and pulled her towards him, his hands cruel on her upper arms, almost jerking her out of the seat. He kissed her, biting at her mouth, then took advantage of her gasp of pain to thrust his tongue deep into her mouth, making her gag with revulsion. At the same time his hand thrust down between her thighs, groping in a manner as disgusting as it was intrusive.

Sheer shock kept Eden frozen, but as soon as his grip slackened she wrenched herself free of him and scrabbled for the door.

He had to be much drunker than she suspected, because although he grabbed for her she managed to fling herself free, scraping her knees as she landed on the gravel. Instinct propelled her through the screen of willow leaves and down the bank, across the little creek and into the welcome sanctuary of another huge old willow.

Without thinking, she shinned up the trunk, hoping fervently that he wouldn't notice the movement of the leaves. The bubbling, chattering little creek hid the noise of her escape and the panting gasps of breath she couldn't quite silence.

'Eden!' he yelled suddenly, from close beneath her.

She shrank back against the trunk, hoping that he wouldn't think to look up.

'Eden, all *right*, I'm sorry, I screwed up. Come back, and I'll take you home!'

For a moment she hesitated, but she didn't trust him. It wouldn't take her long to walk the three miles home, whereas Tod was an unknown factor. In spite of his apparent soberness he had to be fairly drunk, and the drunk were unpredictable. Every instinct was insisting she press herself up against the cool bark of the willow tree and not even breathe.

'All right, then,' he said thickly, startling her anew, 'bloody well walk home, you stupid little slut!'

Eden waited until she heard the car roar off down the road in a spatter of small stones, then lowered herself carefully and gingerly down the tree. It was a lot harder to get down than it had been to get up. The sick panic in her stomach had eased a little; now she just felt sick and cold.

Moving silently, she made her way back across the creek, wincing once when she slipped on a mossy stone and her foot went into the icy water. The little ballet slippers had been good to dance in, but they certainly weren't made for walking or getting wet.

Very cautiously she peeped out from the veil of willow branches, looking carefully both ways. Although she was certain she had heard the car go back down the road, he could have hidden it among the heaps of stone-chips and be lying in wait for her.

But there was no sign of Tod, or the car, and, after a long, silent reconnaissance, she relaxed.

The three miles home were the longest miles she had ever walked. Not only did every stone make itself too obvious through the thin soles of her shoes, but, in spite of the fast pace she set, within minutes she was shivering with cold. A couple of times she had to leap off the road and into the shadow of the trees when a car came by.

Neither of the drivers were Tod, and both would have given her a ride home, but by the time she recognised the vehicles it was too late.

Anyway, something fastidious and proud shrank at the thought of being discovered like this, walking home in such a state. Logic told her that Tod was entirely to blame, but she couldn't help wondering whether she had somehow sent off signals that had made him believe she was promiscuous. There had been, after all, that other leering man who had tried to waylay her.

She was past shivering when she finally made it to the homestead. Her breath was coming fast and shallow to her lungs, and she couldn't even summon up the energy to feel relief. The clink of chains as the dogs came out to inspect her made her start.

'G-good boys,' she said hurriedly. She didn't want them to wake the house.

They were excellent watch-dogs, but fortunately it wasn't her they were protecting the place from. One swiped her hand with a warm tongue, then all four retired back into their kennels.

Moving as quietly as she could, she made her way up the path and on to the veranda, not even looking towards the big bay window that indicated Blade's bedroom.

Once they had never locked the homestead, but those days, alas, were gone. Nevertheless Eden usually slept with her windows wide open. Stumbling a little, she stepped over the sill, and caught back a little sobbing noise when her toes hit the wood. Heart thudding, she froze. But the house was still and quiet except for the usual creaks and groans as it settled down for the night.

But she couldn't stop the uncontrollable shuddering. Her feet were in agony and the cold seemed to have eaten into her bones. She also felt unclean, tarnished by that awful kiss and the way Tod had so roughly manhandled her. Nightgown in hand, she tiptoed silently along to the bathroom, and showered until she was warm again, but nothing could take away the tenderness of her abused lips, or the black wretchedness in her heart.

Huddled in her nightgown, she sneaked back down the passage to her room.

But she stopped just inside the door, her heart drumming in her throat. Blade was standing by the bookcase. As she came in he turned his head, and something about the flat, lethal blue stare warned her before he asked in a soft, silky voice, 'Where have you been?'

The muscles in her throat clamped tight so that she was unable to answer.

'It's almost two-thirty,' he remarked, still in that same chilling monotone. 'What the hell have you been doing?'

'Nothing,' she croaked. He looked as though he wanted to kill her, as though he was keeping control over his emotions by such an immense effort of will that any tiny slip could lead to a breach, and once that was done she would be defenceless in the naked force of his fury. Eden had never been really afraid before, but she knew now what it was like: a kick in the stomach, an acrid, coppery taste in the mouth.

'Don't lie to me.' He came over and stared at her bruised lips. 'I can see what you've been doing.'

Hypnotised by the chilling ferocity in his face, his voice, Eden shook her head. 'I wanted to come home early because I was getting a headache but I—Tod thought——'

'What did Tod think?'

'I asked to come home, and he thought that I wanted to—to park. He stopped at the metal dump. I ran away, and then I had to walk home, but——' The words dried in her mouth as she saw comprehension flame blackly in his expression.

Each lean, strong hand flexed into a cupped curve, into a weapon of destruction by Blade's side. He stood very still in the classic stance of an aggressor, taking several seconds to ask with no inflexion, 'What did he do to you?'

'He kissed me, that's all,' she said swiftly, her eyes swallowing up her thin face. 'I got out of the car and hid up the willow tree—when he parked down in the council depot I was nearly asleep, I thought we were home—but when I ran he said—he said he'd take me home. But I wasn't going to take the chance, so I lay low. In the end he drove away. Then I climbed down and walked home.'

A tremendous shiver shook her. Instantly his arm came around her. He was so warm, so strong.

'He bruised your mouth,' he said silkily.

With a soundless sigh she surrendered, leaning against him. 'I think he must have been drunk,' she confided, yawning, shaking with reaction. 'But he didn't seem to be; he was drinking rum, but I didn't see him drinking much, and he wasn't slurring like some of the others, and he could walk straight. I didn't know, otherwise I'd have rung you . . .'

'Shh. Don't worry about it now.' His voice was deep in his chest so that she felt it as well as heard it. 'Are you all right?'

'Yes.' Now that that terrifying fury seemed to have faded Eden wasn't going to risk it again by telling him about her sore feet. 'I'm sorry I woke you up.'

He laughed. 'You didn't.' When she yawned again he said softly, 'Are you sure you're all right? You feel as though you could still be in shock.'

'Of c-course I'm all right.' She rested her cheek against the smooth material of his dressing-gown. She could hear his heartbeat, steady, strong, the pulse of life. A massive shiver took her by surprise, and to her horror and surprise tears stung her eyes. She fought them back, but a sob caught in her throat.

Instantly Blade ordered, 'Get into bed. I put the electric blanket on when I came in, so you could get warm quickly.'

He lifted her and thrust her between the sheets. She tried to smile at him, but tears clogged her throat, even though she clenched her jaw to stop them.

'Eden,' he murmured softly.

The bed depressed as he sat down. She gave a convulsive shudder and whispered, 'I'm sorry; I don't know what's the matter with me. I'll be all right.' But the tears kept coming and gave the lie to her assertion.

'You've had a scare,' he said grimly, 'and walked three miles home on a dark, quite chilly night. You have every right to a few tears.'

'I don't cry very often.' But she was crying now—not sobbing; it was just that the tears wouldn't stop. 'Don't go away,' she muttered, appalling herself with the involuntary plea.

He hesitated, and she was racked with humiliation, but after a moment he said calmly, 'Move over.'

She scrubbed at her eyes, despising herself for her weakness, and he came down beside her, scooping her on to his shoulder so that his heat encompassed her. Sheer shock dried the tears; she lifted her face as he said calmly, 'Just go to sleep, all right? You need something to take your mind off what happened.'

And he kissed her, gently, yet with enough firmness to keep her still when she flinched away. But this was nothing like that repulsive kiss Tod had forced on her. This was Blade, and she loved him. The misery and embarrassment fled in an incandescent rush of pleasure.

Slowly, insensibly, she relaxed, letting the magic of his mouth, his presence, knit together the confidence and the self-esteem she had lost. Even when he touched her tender lower lip with his tongue, she trusted him enough to open at the silent summons.

He was careful not to hurt her anew, but he kissed her very thoroughly, and, when at last he lifted his head and said, 'Now, go to sleep,' she was flushed and warm all over, her eyes heavy-lidded and slumbrous, her mouth cherished, all memories of Tod's assault fled.

Exhaustion drugged her. She couldn't even lift her head. Another shudder shook her, and she sighed and went to sleep.

In the morning she woke alone, but Blade's faint, teasing scent, salty, quintessentially male, clung to her sheets and pillows. She would never, she thought, smoothing the pillow with a tremulous smile, be able to sleep in the bed again without remembering that she had spent the night in Blade's arms.

Something fluttery and heated unfurled in the pit of her stomach, sending messages through her body. She was elated, yet afraid, and she didn't know how she was going to meet his eyes.

It was nine o'clock before she got up; a quick glance at the mirror revealed that her swollen lips had softened a little, but the bruise was still there. Anger darkened her gaze, turning it turbulent green. How dared Tod think that he could do that to her? Drunk or not, he had no right to touch her. Had it been anything she had said or done that had convinced him he could handle her so cruelly?

But, no; she had certainly danced with him, and talked to him, laughed with him, but she was sure she hadn't been openly provocative. And even if she had, once she had said no he should have stopped. Still fuming, she went along to the kitchen, and made a pot of tea and a piece of toast. The telephone rang, but it must have been a wrong number, because no one spoke on the other end. Shrugging, she hung up.

Blade came in just as she was washing her mug and plate. Carefully she set them on the rack before she acknowledged his arrival. Even in his working clothes he looked magnificent, the sleeves rolled up to expose strong arms, the trousers clinging to his thighs and hips.

'How are you?' he asked, watching her keenly.

She produced a smile. 'I'm fine.'

He strolled over and tipped her chin, scanning her face. Fascinated, she coloured at the touch of his finger around her lips, and watched as his eyes grew cold. 'The bastard!' he rasped, half below his breath.

She said hastily, 'It's all right, truly it is.'

'Do you want to prosecute him?'

She went white. 'I—I hadn't even thought of it. But it's only his word against mine, isn't it?'

'He might manage to rape the next girl he takes out.'

There came a sick resurgence of fear, and Blade swore and hauled her close. For a long moment Eden let herself lean on him, dazzled by the heat of him, the hard power of his body against her.

'Do you think I should?' she asked docilely.

'No,' he decided after a moment. 'As you say, it's your word against his. I'll deal with it.'

Startled, she pulled away to stare up into the face carved into implacable lines. 'You'll deal with it? How?'

'I'll deal with *him*,' he said calmly, putting her off. 'You're the one who has to deal with the results of the attack. Are you sure you're OK?'

She flushed a little. 'I'm fine. Thank you for being so kind last night. I needed to know that—that I could be close to someone and not——' her colour deepened and she was a little taken aback by the icy control that held his features locked, but she ploughed on '—not have to worry. I needed comfort, and that's what you gave me,' she finished, adding a little desperately, 'I was afraid that men only wanted one thing, and it was—wonderful to realise that you didn't.'

There was a taut moment before he smiled without humour, and said negligently, 'Any time, Eden. Not all men are young and stupid and brash, too drunk to control themselves.'

# CHAPTER SIX

A COUPLE of hours later Eden was appalled to almost fall over Tod as she came in from the garden with an armful of blood-red Ena Harkness roses, seeking to comfort her lacerated self-esteem with their wondrous scent. He was standing outside the back door, obviously preparing to force himself to knock, and when she said his name on a shocked, indrawn breath he swung around, jaw braced, his expression a mixture of arrogance and shame and sulkiness.

'I came to apologise,' he said angrily. The attacker of the night before turned suddenly into a spoiled, uncertain young man.

'All right.' Eden was rather pleased to hear that her voice was steady. It almost helped to make up for the inadequacy of her reply.

He flushed. 'Oh, hell!' he exclaimed, glowering. 'I had too much to drink, damn it, but you—you made me wild!'

'Why?'

His colour deepened. He looked at her as though he hated her. 'Because you so very clearly didn't give a damn,' he said sullenly. 'I thought you were leading me on.'

Anger sharpened her voice as she demanded, 'How, for heaven's sake?'

'Hell, you looked like—well, I don't have to tell you you're pretty; you know that. And you dance like a dream. I thought it was for me, but it wasn't, was it?'

The sick fear had gone, and with it a load she hadn't even been aware she was bearing. 'No,' she said, more gently. 'I wanted to look nice, but it wasn't a come-on.'

He didn't shuffle his feet, but she decided it was only because his pride wouldn't let him. 'Why the hell did you say you'd come out with me if you weren't interested?' he demanded.

'Because I liked you. Because I wanted to go to the party.' Blade's savage suggestion that he might rape the next girl who said no haunted her. For the sake of that next girl she said, 'But taking me to a party doesn't entitle you to anything but the pleasure of my company, you know.'

He stared at her, his eyes unable to leave the swollen contours of her mouth. 'You sound like my mother. Oh, hell, she's right and so are you. I'm sorry,' he muttered. 'I suppose I've done my chances well and truly.'

She shrugged, feeling suddenly very much older than him. 'Thank you for coming. It took guts.'

He closed his eyes for a second. 'What else could I do,' he said curtly, 'after your bloody bodyguard appeared up at our house and more or less told me that if I didn't he'd beat the stuffing out of me?'

'Blade?' So that was how he had 'dealt' with him. Pure naked aggression.

'Yes.' Tod looked embarrassed. 'I mean—well, I knew I'd blown it, that you weren't that sort of girl, but I doubt whether I'd have had the guts to come and say I was sorry. Not cold.'

She liked Tod more at that moment of revelation than she had ever before. 'Well, you've apologised now,' she said gently. 'It's all right.'

He nodded, but added, as though he wanted her to know, 'I wouldn't have—made you, you know. It was just—I mean, you are different, and the first time I saw you I thought you were great, and—well, I knew you'd turned down just about everyone else around, so I thought that meant you liked me...'

He stopped, stuffing his hands in his pockets only to remove them almost immediately, looking like an aggrieved small boy. It was clear that he was not accustomed to explaining his actions, or even considering them. But he went on doggedly, 'Then you said no, and I lost my head and grabbed. I thought you'd been having me on. I suppose I wanted to teach you a lesson. Then you ran, and I realised—well, I felt angry and sick and ashamed too, so I stormed off.' He fixed her with an accusing stare. 'I spent the night worrying myself sick in case you hadn't made it home. I rang this morning, and when I heard your voice I hung up.'

So that was the phone call.

'To see that you were all right,' he explained, some of his assurance returning. 'And then Hammond turned up. Hell, I thought he was going to kill me!'

He stopped, but when she said nothing he went on, 'I suppose I should be thankful he didn't tell my parents. But he's bloody unsparing—he's got a tongue like a chain-saw. Not,' he added defiantly, 'that he needed to say what he did. I was feeling pretty damned sick, I can tell you, and not just with a hangover. I've never done anything like that before.'

He'd never had to, Eden guessed. He had probably always relied on his charm and good looks and his powers of persuasion to get him what he wanted. She said, 'It's all right; there was no harm done.'

Clearly he wanted to say more, but she didn't want to hear it, and after a moment he nodded and said stiffly, 'All right, catch you later.'

Sam was walking slowly out to his favourite chair on the veranda when she came out after putting the roses in water. 'Recovered from the night's debaucheries?' he asked, with a grin.

She tried to laugh it off. 'Yes, although I feel a little stiff. All that dancing.'

'I don't call it dancing,' he returned promptly. 'Gyrating like dervishes, more like.'

He walked much more slowly than he had even a month or so ago, and it took a considerable amount of care and time to lower himself into his chair. After

picking the beans, Eden sat down beside him and spent
the rest of the morning with him, her hands flying as
she sliced the beans. Nobody came near them, for which
she was devoutly thankful.

That evening she walked out into the hall and heard
Blade say, 'Hello, darling,' in a voice she had never heard
him use before.

He was speaking to Thea, and, as the phone hadn't
rung, he must have contacted her.

It was like a blow to the heart. Compelled by the
tearing pain, Eden sublimated the black bitterness of
jealousy by hoeing in the vegetable garden until dusk
solidified into a crystal night and the mosquitoes' insistence drove her inside.

On her way back in she met Blade. Of course, she
thought despairingly as she nodded unsmilingly at him.
She knew she had several smudges on her cheeks where
she had swatted intrusive insects, and sweat caked her
hair, turning it into strings about her face.

'On Friday, would you make up a bed in the room
next to mine?' he asked without preamble, very much
master of the house. 'Thea's coming up to spend the
weekend here. She'll arrive about nine, so organise some
sort of supper for her as well. You won't have to cook
a meal for us on Saturday night because we're going out
to dinner. And she'll be leaving just after lunch on
Sunday. OK?'

Eden nodded, because there was nothing else she could
do. She might even have said something, but she had no
memory of it later, when she crouched under the shower
so that the tears could run uninterrupted and unheard
down her face.

But, as she lay the long hours of night through in her
bed, she came to a conclusion. She had foolishly allowed the crush she was suffering to escalate into love,
but everyone knew that first love never lasted. So all she
had to do was wait it out, and eventually this desolate

ache in her heart would go and she would be able to look Blade in the eyes without a pang of grief or pain.

It just took time. And she would have to pin on a smile even if it killed her.

She wished that she had had a more normal up-bringing, one where she would have gone to school and met boys, whether in the classroom or as brothers of her friends. Then she would have cut her emotional teeth on someone a lot less enigmatic and complex than Blade. She would know how to cope with such a head-over-heels, run-away extravaganza of emotion. Experience would have rendered her less naïve; in other words, the situation would be a little easier, a little less traumatic.

But she had no experience, and nothing to cling to but this pride she had so lately developed. Gritting her teeth, Eden prayed that it would be enough to get her through.

Hard common sense, developed over these last years, forced her to see beyond her own anguish, and view the future practically. If Blade married—and inevitably he would—there would be no place for her and her grand-father on Onemahutu.

Tomorrow she would go into town and harry the ac-countant. It was vital that she know just what their situ-ation was.

But, if they left, would that dump her grandfather back into the old depression, the slow waiting for death?

It was so unfair, she wailed silently, tossing in her bed. Why did people have to die, grow old and weak? But after a few moments of self-pity she pushed the debili-tating emotion to the back of her mind, and began to plan. They would have to buy a house, and she would need a job. That would mean leaving her grandfather alone at home all day, but she had had to do that before Blade had arrived back on the scene. They had managed.

Only, Sam was weaker now than he had been then. Cold fear clutched her heart, was banished. She could not afford to give in to it. She would make her plans as best she could, and as soon as they knew they would start the desperate process of untangling their hearts from Onemahutu.

On Monday she took the car into Kaikohe, bought groceries, and went to see the accountant. Looking over his spectacles at her, he listened to her carefully, then took some time to formulate an answer.

'As far as I can see,' he said carefully, 'you are not going to come out of this with any more than twenty thousand dollars. At the most.'

Eden's breath was sucked into her chest. 'But that's not enough to buy a section, let alone a house!' she exclaimed hoarsely.

He shook his head. 'No. You'll have to rent.'

She clenched her shaking hands in her lap. 'You're sure that's all?'

'I can go into all the figures, but, to put it succinctly, yes, that's all.' He looked away from her face, shuffling papers about on his desk, and, perhaps to give her time to collect herself, explained again what he had told her several times before. 'I'm afraid your grandfather borrowed more than he could repay. He didn't foresee the great drop in prices for primary products, and he used the money to do a great many non-productive things as well as developing Onemahutu.'

Non-productive, of course, meant the refurbishing of the houses, especially the huge amount of money that had been spent on the homestead. And the holidays overseas. And the lavish entertainment.

'The only thing that's stopped a mortgagor stepping in is the fact that you've been earning just enough to service the debts,' the accountant told her gently. 'But now that the place is sold, the principal has to be paid. And that will leave you with almost nothing, because of course Onemahutu is not worth nearly as much as it was ten years ago, when your grandfather took out the last loan.'

Eden nodded, fighting panic with stiff stubbornness. 'I'll have to think, to plan,' she said quietly, getting to her feet.

'I'll be happy to help,' the accountant began.

But she shook her head. 'No, there are things I have to take into consideration,' she said vaguely, wondering what on earth they could do. If they left Onemahutu it would be with only enough money to rent a house for five years or so. After that the money would run out.

Summoning a pale smile, she left, walking down the stairs with her future darkening by the step in front of her. She had no skill or talent or qualifications that would help her earn. Any job she was able to get would be paid at the most basic level.

Once she had dreamed of going to university; in fact, her mother had left her a small legacy so that she could, but she was going to have to use that to help provide some sort of home for her grandfather. She had saved every possible cent from the salary Blade was paying her, but it was a pitifully small amount, too small to make any difference.

Of course, whispered temptation, if you stayed a year or so, you'd have lots more.

And do you have any right, her conscience intervened, to drag Grandad away, when he's happy again?

As she drove the big car home, Eden hardened her heart, realising how much she had let Blade's offer of a home and job sap her initiative. Wishful thinking had clouded her brain to the stage where she was content to let someone else make decisions for her. She should have insisted on making her own...

Blade came out to help her carry in the groceries, and she felt a rush of delight that frightened her anew. She was too aware of him, too attuned to his sheer physical magic, always sneaking covert glances at him, wholly enchanted by his splendid male grace and presence. That, of course, was one of the reasons she'd have to go. It would be plain stupidity to prolong this situation when she was so vulnerable.

Whether or not he loved Thea, he certainly did not love Eden!

But, oh, the thought of leaving him was like bitter pain, cold and slow and aching through the years. Until she came up with some sort of plan for the future, they had to stay. So she would have to avoid Blade as much as possible. It would be utterly foolish to pack up with nothing organised, possible even dangerous for her grandfather.

It wasn't too difficult to do. She had to share her meals with him, of course, but most of the time she was able to stay well out of his way. She developed the habit of leaving him with Sam after dinner so that they could talk. It hurt, because she had enjoyed being with them, taking part in the conversation, but now she stayed only a few minutes before making some excuse and sliding out of the room.

Some of the lengthening evenings she spent working in the vegetable garden until it grew dark, then read in her bedroom, occasionally watching television to give her weary mind some rest. Usually around nine-thirty, just before her grandfather went to bed, she brought them in a hot drink, beef tea for her grandfather, coffee for Blade.

It was on one such evening midway through the week that she heard her grandfather's voice as she came quietly across the grass.

'. . . haven't got much longer to go,' he said, not so much wearily as with resignation, 'and to be quite honest with you, Blade, I don't want to stay. I'm tired. But I can't leave Eden as things are.'

Blade said something, and her grandfather snorted.

'She's a good girl, but she knows about as much of the world as a new-born babe! I wouldn't rest easy if I thought she was alone in the world. It's been worrying me. She always was a delicate little thing, but I think perhaps I should have insisted she go off to school like all the other children, and then at least she might have friends. As it is, she has no one.'

Eden was cold, shivering, but she couldn't move.

'So what do you want from me?' Blade asked, his voice slow and deliberate, almost drawling.

'I want to know that you'll take care of her. Make sure she isn't left alone when I die.'

There was a second's silence, then Blade said calmly, 'You know I'll do that.'

Her grandfather sounded satisfied. 'Yes, I was pretty sure you would, but I had to be certain.'

They hadn't pulled the curtains, and to Eden's horror she saw Blade's silhouette as he rose and came towards the window. Breaking free of the dismay that had kept her feet nailed to the ground, she whirled away and disappeared around the corner of the house, her mouth trembling with a mixture of pain and rage.

How dared Sam hand her on to someone else, as though she were totally witless and incompetent? And how dared Blade accept that charge, treating her like a favourite pet whose welfare was causing some concern?

Wondering desperately why her grandfather thought he had so little time left to live, she hurtled through the french window and into her bedroom. For long moments she stood in the darkening room, hands clenched as she worried. Outrage and fear and a deep, panicky grief mingled, prohibiting rational thought.

But gradually she calmed down. Sam saw women as the frailer sex, dependent upon men for their welfare, so she shouldn't blame him for an attitude he had held all his life. And Blade, she thought with her mouth turned down and her heart melting in her, well, Blade was the sort of man whose instincts were pretty old-fashioned too, however out of date that was at the moment.

As for her grandfather's conviction that he had little time left... Tears burned behind Eden's eyes, thickened in her throat. 'No,' she whispered, daring him to be right.

He had probably just had an uncomfortable day. Or perhaps he was using that as a little lever to get Blade to promise. Her thoughts raced round and round, seeking some solution to a situation that was becoming more and more untenable.

She understood why her grandfather had done it. All his life he had looked after the women in his family as best as he could, and he was simply making sure that, when he was no longer able to, someone he trusted would still do so.

That was the reason he had gone downhill so fast when Eden had been working the property, and why he had been so much better since Blade had come on the scene.

He didn't comprehend women's desire for independence, although he understood that, for those unfortunate enough not to have men to protect them, it was a necessary thing. He was an unregenerate chauvinist, and it was too late for him to change now.

That was why he and Blade got on so well together, because Eden suspected that Blade, too, considered men to be the natural guardians of any women about.

It was an old-fashioned attitude, but one she understood. And, although she had every intention of carving out her own future when she had to leave Onemahutu, she couldn't prevent the warm glow of confidence it gave her to know that Blade had promised to look after her.

So perhaps, she thought, smiling wryly, she too was a little old-fashioned in her outlook.

But she frowned almost immediately, for of course she couldn't plan to leave Onemahutu now—not after she had heard Grandad say he had little time left. Even if he *was* wrong—'And he *is*,' she said stoutly—it would be nothing short of cruelty to drag him away.

She sat down on the side of her bed and put her head in her hands, trapped, trying to work out what she could do.

Thea Gardiner was tall and blonde and chic, with a magnificent body, long, long legs, a narrow waist, and a deep, lush bust. She wasn't beautiful, but so impressive was her personality and her appearance that Eden didn't notice for some time that her features weren't perfect and her large eyes were just a little too close together. She was, Eden decided dismally, a finished, polished work of art.

And she was in love with Blade. There was no mistaking that; she hung on his every word as though he were the only man in the world, flirted with him, fluttered dark lashes at him, gazed at him with her bold blue eyes as though she wanted to carry him off there and then.

It was difficult to see what Blade thought of this open parade of emotions; he was as reserved as ever, but he smiled at Thea with something more than affection, and he certainly didn't object to the way she clung to his arm or cuddled up to him.

It didn't help matters to discover that she was charming, too.

'So you're the pretty voice,' she said, smiling, when she was introduced to Eden. 'How nice to have a face to go with it!'

It was said kindly, but made Eden feel as though she were still at primary school. However, although she felt uncomfortable with the woman, she had to admit that Thea was as much fun as she was stunning. She pulled her weight in the house, she flirted with Sam, responding to his old-fashioned gallantry with aplomb and appreciation, she was clever and quick-witted, and she enjoyed herself.

All in all, the perfect house guest.

Eden found herself liking her, although Thea had a tendency to treat her as though she were a sweet but slightly simple-minded younger sister, which would have antagonised her enormously if she'd let it. But at least, she thought drearily as she lay in bed on the Friday night, she now had no illusions about her own attraction.

Compared to the older woman she was about as exciting as cold mutton. Thea was clever and sophisticated and witty, with a quick answer to any comment, and a wide knowledge of books and films and plays. She wore her clothes with a panache that would outshine most women, let alone a country mouse!

An hour later Eden was still lying wide awake, trying not to listen to the house noises, in case one of them should be the sound of people moving about from one bedroom to another. A shattering sob hurt her chest. She could not bear to lie there and wonder, to imagine them together. In the bathroom cabinet were a few ancient sleeping-pills. She took one, and was pathetically grateful when she felt the waves of sleep drag her under.

Gratitude was not her emotion when she awoke the next morning, however, with a dry mouth and a thud in her head that threatened to develop into a headache. She showered, and was walking back to her room when she heard Thea's distinctive low chuckle, only seconds before the woman came out of the door to Blade's bedroom.

She stopped when she saw Eden looking at her, and her mouth quirked in a wry smile. 'Well, I told him it was a waste of time getting you to make up a bed for me,' she said with an odd little smile, 'but, like all truly strong men, Blade's protective. I think he feels you should be sheltered from the—er—more raunchy aspects of life.'

From somewhere Eden dredged up enough poise to shrug. Thea was wearing a pale blue sundress, cinched tightly around her narrow waist to show off her magnificent breasts. She looked tempestuous enough to be exciting, yet essentially wholesome.

'I don't really think I need to be sheltered,' Eden said huskily, listening to the sound of her heart breaking, 'but it's kind of him to try.'

Thea beamed at her. 'He's a darling, as well as being about the most sexy man on earth!' she agreed cordially, falling into step beside Eden. 'Women fall over themselves to fall in love with him, you know, because he's so nice.'

Had she realised, and was she, in her own way, trying to make Eden feel a little better? Eden went cold at the thought, but managed to say in a reasonably steady voice, 'Lucky man.'

'Lucky me, I think. See you at breakfast.' Thea gave her a wink and went into the room that had been designated hers.

Eden didn't cry. Her pain went too deep for that. She went cautiously into her bedroom, as though moving might snap her in two, and stood looking down at the photograph of her mother on the dressing-table. Was this how Linda had felt when her lover had died, as though nothing in the world was going to be right again? She had never looked at another man, never even thought of going out with one. 'Oh, God,' Eden whispered, 'I hope I'm not like that. At least Linda had a baby to love...'

For a moment she thought she might fling herself down on the floor and howl, but she gave her mother's laughing face a final glance, and straightened up. Linda had coped, and so would she.

In fact, she was rather surprised at how well she coped. She didn't burst into tears when she saw Thea's radiant face over the breakfast table, nor did she look reproachfully at Blade's enigmatic countenance. She tried very hard to be her usual self, and succeeded well enough, she hoped, to fool anyone.

Afterwards Thea helped her clear up, waiting until the dishwasher had been set before saying tentatively, 'Blade tells me you had a rather unpleasant experience last weekend.'

Shamed colour touched Eden's cheeks, then fled. She looked at this woman, ripe and lovely as the day, met her sympathetic eyes, and forced back the humiliation and the bitter flash of betrayal. How could he have told her?

But she replied evenly, 'Yes, I did.'

'God, some men!' Thea astonished Eden by giving her a quick hug. 'Some men think they have a God-given right to maul any woman who catches their eye. But they're not all like that, so don't worry about it; don't let it put you off the male sex.'

Eden gave her a pale smile. 'I won't,' she said, wishing that the older woman weren't so likeable.

'Blade thought you might need a woman to talk to,' Thea went on, getting down a cup and saucer. 'I think I'll have another cup of coffee. Want some? No? No, don't you do it; I can see where things are.'

'That's kind of him—and of you—but really, I'm OK. Tod's just a spoilt kid. He wasn't really dangerous—I think I probably over-reacted.'

Thea looked at her, suddenly very serious. 'There's no such thing as over-reacting,' she said steadily. 'If you *feel* threatened, you *are* threatened. You did the right thing.'

Eden winced. So Blade had told her everything—no doubt even that she had begged him to stay with her that night.

But if he had, Thea didn't mention it. Her voice was a little muffled as she continued, 'If you want to talk about it, feel free. All women have tales of horror to swap!'

Eden replied, 'I suppose so.'

'Unfortunately there are few men around like Blade. That basic goodness,' Thea went on cheerfully, 'is one of the reasons so many women fall in love with him, you know. And the other, I think, is because essentially he's totally untamed. We wonder just what exciting, dangerous things lie beneath that wonderfully controlled surface, and ask ourselves whether we can possibly be the one to make him lose that armour of restraint. It's a fascinating quest.'

'The coffee's in the fridge,' Eden said calmly.

Thea emerged from the depths of the fridge, waving the container of coffee beans triumphantly. 'But most men are decent sorts, you know. I'd be prepared to bet that even your over-enthusiastic swain of last weekend is quite a nice chap at heart. He just needs to be told in no uncertain terms that he has no right to assume anything about a woman, and that every woman has the right to call a halt when and where and at the time she wants to.'

'Of course you're right,' Eden agreed tonelessly. Fortunately Thea said no more, so she was able to go about her housework while Thea sat with Sam out on the veranda; she could just hear the sounds of their laughter as she moved about getting lunch ready.

No doubt Blade had been thinking only of her welfare when he'd told Thea about Tod. No doubt they had been entwined in the huge kauri bed, flushed and sated in the lassitude of satisfied desire when he'd told her. Humiliation corroded Eden's pride into dust. Fiercely she fought it down. She was not going to get through this weekend by giving in to her emotions, and she had to appear as normal as possible, for her own sake as well as Sam's.

For a moment anguish speared through Eden, so intense that she had to grip the bench. She could not bear to think of Thea and Blade—but she must accept it, she had to; there was absolutely nothing she could do about it. No one had ever died of a broken heart. But oh, it hurt.

Blade was an enigma—so kind, and then betraying her to Thea, so gentle with her, so brutal to Tod that he'd terrified him into apologising. A cold little chill pulled her skin tight. What sort of man had the will-power to keep such intense emotions restrained by the leash of his self-discipline?

A man she had no hope of understanding. Such ruthless constraint was frightening. What other emotions burned with white-hot intensity deep in his heart?

As she scrubbed the small new potatoes and set them to cook with mint and butter, she mulled over this aspect of his personality. Had she been as experienced as Thea, she would have understood him better, realising that no man could possess that fierce attraction without the ca-pacity to feel a corresponding depth of emotion.

She had been too naïve.

The story of my life, she thought sourly as she set the table. Too naïve to understand that Tod might look at her innocent attempts to dress up, and see provocation, unable to see past the golden mask of Blade's self-possession to the leashed emotions beneath.

Her hands settled, slowed, as she set down the knives and forks. Last weekend she had seen another facet of Blade's complex character—his understanding that she had needed comfort and the presence of another person. His undemanding closeness had restored some basic confidence in her that Tod's angry attack had shattered.

Small tingles of heat pulled through her. She set the salt and pepper sets down with a shaking hand, recalling the soft texture of his body hair against her cheek, silk over satin, and the hard bulge of muscles across his chest, the way his legs had warmed hers, the touch of his hand on her waist, calm, firm, immensely comforting.

That was what it was like to lie with a man. There had been nothing sexual at all in his touch, but he knew how to handle a woman, he knew that he was attractive. A bitter envy darkened her eyes. Lucky Thea. To know that when he lay in bed with her it was not just to give the matchless security of his presence, but because he wanted her. Eden would give—almost everything—to know that, and it was unlikely ever to happen, because he thought her a child.

As, compared to Thea, she was.

She got through the rest of the weekend on a combination of nerves and stiff pride and acting ability. Watching them go out on Saturday night was a severe test of all three, but she smiled as they left at last, Thea provocatively beautiful in a black lace dress that emphasised her opulent attractions, Blade more than a match for her. Eden's hungry eyes devoured him. He looked superb in evening clothes, wearing them with a worldly, understated elegance that pointed up his cool, arrogant masculinity.

Eden took another sleeping-pill that night, once again waking headachy and dry-mouthed. Disgusted with herself, she flushed the three remaining tablets away.

Blade had breakfast with her. In spite of her covert glances she could see no evidence of a passionate night in his face, and she was disgusted anew with herself for trying to find any.

Wearily relieved that he took Thea out in the Land Rover later in the morning, Eden went out to pick a lettuce and some beans for lunch. It was hot, and she emptied her mind of all the turmoil, letting the peace, the scent of the earth and green, growing things, the lazy breath of the warm breeze, soak into her.

She returned to the homestead convinced that she had the strength to deal with her misery. It would not be easy, but she could do it. All she had to do was take a deep breath and let things wash over her.

'What are we having for lunch?'

She changed direction and went across to the veranda, where Sam sat watching the antics of two small kittens with a tolerant eye. 'Bacon and egg pie, beans, new potatoes and salad,' she told him. 'I'll just put these away and then I'll bring the beans out and do them here.'

It was a lazy half-hour she spent with him; they didn't talk much, but the silences were filled with amusement as the two kittens tumbled like small ginger balls over their feet.

But eventually Eden got up, saying, 'I'd better go, I suppose. Blade wants lunch at twelve sharp.'

'I like my lunch at twelve sharp, too,' her grandfather said slyly. One of the kittens had crawled up into his lap, and his gnarled old hand was stroking it gently. As she left he was already sliding into the light doze that came so often and so easily to him now.

She was pulling the bacon and egg pie from the oven when Blade came in.

He said her name, but she knew. 'Grandad?' she whispered.

'Yes,' he said sombrely, his expression bleak and controlled. 'I'm afraid so. I've rung the doctor, but there's no hope, Eden.'

He held out his hand, and she put her cold one in it and went out with him on to the veranda, where her grandfather sat just as though he had gone to sleep. He looked peaceful, even pleased, as though he had been enjoying a happy dream when he died.

Eden bent and kissed his forehead, then, eyes dry and burning, let Thea lead her back to the sitting-room and give her brandy and tea while Blade used the telephone.

She didn't take much in, although she obediently ate some of the lunch she had prepared, and even helped Thea clear away; but it wasn't until quite late that evening, when the last of the kindly neighbours with their offerings of food and help, and their deep, mostly unspoken sympathy, had gone, that she realised Thea was no longer there.

'She had to go back down to Auckland,' Blade explained. He was being very gentle with her. 'She has to present a proposal tomorrow. Do you want someone else? Mrs Clare?'

'No.' Nobody could ease this frightening emptiness in her heart. She asked, 'Did you contact my godmother?'

'I tried to. Apparently she's walking around Tuscany, but——'

'Don't bring her back,' Eden said quietly. She didn't need anyone else but Blade. All of her outrage had gone; she was glad now that her grandfather had asked him to look after her. With Blade she would be quite safe.

In the following awful days Eden relied completely on him. He made all the arrangements, gave her constant, undemanding support at the funeral, even managed to track her godmother down in Siena.

'Darling, are you sure you're all right?' Freda asked agitatedly over the telephone. 'Mr Hammond sounds very competent, but I think I'll try to get a ticket home straight away.'

'No, you stay there.' Eden's voice echoed weirdly on the line. 'You've only got another ten days, haven't you? And really, Freda, I don't need you. Blade has been wonderful.'

'Yes,' Freda said doubtfully. 'Eden, when I get back, you must come and stay with me for a little holiday. Oh, I'm so sorry I wasn't there when—— Never mind, keep your chin up, darling, and I'll see you in ten days or so.'

Eden put the receiver down and turned, the first tears blinding her. Almost instantly she was caught and held, cradled close to the matchless comfort of Blade's big body as she wept out the pain and the grief. But it seemed as though something had been broken in her, some vital part of her had been lost.

When after a fortnight she was still moping like a pale wraith around the house, shadows beneath as well as within her eyes, Blade tracked her down to where she sat huddled in her grandfather's chair on the veranda, and said with a crisp lack of mercy, 'Self-pity is an emotion I have very little respect for.'

It was like being slapped in the face. Eden stared at him, her mouth trembling, but there was no hint of the sympathy she relied so much on in his chiselled features.

'I miss him,' she said, wounded, her great green-brown eyes filling with tears.

'I know. So do I. But how do you think he would feel if he could see you like this?'

She bit her trembling lips, looking away from the inexorable judgement in his regard.

Ruthlessly he pursued, 'How do you think he would feel? How would your mother feel? Your grandmother? You're wandering around like a little ghost, demanding compassion, parading your grief like a banner instead of dealing with it and getting on with life. You're spineless, Eden, and that's a pity, because I thought you had more of your grandfather in you. More of your mother too; life dealt her blows that might have crushed a weaker woman, but she took them on the chin and came through.'

Eden's chin lifted automatically. Sparks of dislike flared in the dark depths of her eyes, and her mouth firmed. 'All right,' she said coldly, 'you don't need to hammer it home. I'm sorry I've bored you with my grief; I'll do my best to keep it hidden from now on.'

'Good.' He turned away, then added absently, 'By the way, there was a phone call for you from Sam's solicitor. I made an appointment for you to see him later this afternoon. I'll take you in, so be ready at two-thirty.'

In her bedroom she stood for a moment, looking first at the strong, vibrant face of her mother in the photograph on the dressing-table, and then at her own in the mirror. Her lips and cheeks were pale, her hair needed washing, her neck drooped in a way she knew had become almost a habit. Blade had been unforgivably right. Defiance sparkled for a moment in her lack-lustre expression, but faded as her cheeks grew hot with shamed colour.

After a moment she sat down on the bed. Her grand-father's loss was like a wound in her heart, colouring her life in dull monotones, but she should have realised what she was doing. She *had* been wearing her emotions on her sleeve, wallowing in her grief instead of coping with it. No one, neither her mother nor her grand-parents, would have been proud of her. Blade had been a little crueller than he'd needed to be, but she would not wander around the place like a lost soul any more.

So as soon as she got into the car she said gruffly, 'I'm sorry for being a wet blanket.'

He sent her a swift look, sharp and blue as the blade of a Spanish sword. 'All right,' he said in a tone that was almost offhand. 'Don't worry about it.'

Rebuffed, she stared out through the window. A brisk easterly blew across the hills and valleys, cooling the air, bringing with it the scent of rain. The forecast said another high was approaching across the Tasman, so probably the threat was completely illusory. Fortunately the season had been kind to the north; the farmers had plenty of grass for their animals, and hay crops thick and ready to harvest.

Blade dropped her off outside Mr Sopworthy's offices, saying laconically, 'I'll be back in half an hour or so.'

Firmly repressing a panicky urge to ask him to come in with her, Eden straightened her shoulders and nodded, turning away to climb the stairs to the solicitor's office.

Ten minutes later she was staring at the portly, neatly clad Mr Sopworthy with astonishment. 'Would you like to explain that to me in ordinary English?' she asked through tight lips.

'I didn't like it,' the solicitor said fussily, 'but your grandfather insisted. Put in plain words, whatever is left over when all debts are paid goes into a trust for you, and Blade Hammond has been appointed as sole trustee. You receive the principal when you turn twenty-five, or sooner if he believes that you are mature enough to deal with such an inheritance. In the meantime, Blade can enjoy the use of it, unconditionally.'

She stared at him. 'What does that mean?'

'It means that, although the money is yours, you do not have any control, or gain any advantage from it.' He hesitated, then said more gently, 'It is quite normal, Eden, for some disposition such as this to be made when the beneficiary is young, and unable, in the eyes of the testator, to look after a large sum of money. However, I tried to persuade your grandfather not to give sole control to Mr Hammond, although I have nothing against the man, and I'm sure he will take great care of your money for you.'

Her throat was dry, parched, but slowly common sense reasserted itself. This was exactly how she should have expected Sam to think. When he had asked Blade to look after her he had meant in every way. She gave a little nod. 'But he can give me money from the trust if I need it?'

'Yes, exactly.' Sopworthy hesitated, then said delicately, 'You can, of course, contest the will.'

'No.' Eden shook her head decisively. 'No, I'm sure Grandad knew what he was doing when he asked Blade to be trustee. Thank you,' she said, getting to her feet so that he wouldn't notice the tell-tale quiver of her lips. 'You've been very kind.'

He frowned, watching her closely. 'Don't hesitate to contact me if you need help,' he told her.

'Thank you.' She went out into the cloudy cool day, pulling her jacket around her as the wind hurtled around the corner of the buildings and plucked at the material.

Blade was waiting in the car, apparently watching people as they went up and down the street, but when she got back into the car he blinked, as though he had been a long way away.

'I believe you are my trustee now,' she said steadily.

'Yes.'

She cast him an uncertain glance, but his profile was etched in steel as he put the car into gear, the slight malformation of his broken nose giving him a brutal air she had never noticed before.

'What will we do?' she asked, suddenly uncertain.

He didn't look away from the road. 'You,' he said unemotionally, 'will go down to stay with your godmother. I've already spoke to her about it, and she's more than happy to have you.'

'Yes, but when I come back——'

'Eden, you won't be coming back.'

She didn't believe her ears. 'What——?'

'You are not coming back. Onemahutu is mine; there is no place for you there now.' He spoke evenly, as though he didn't care that her heart was being shredded, as though she meant nothing to him.

Her stunned eyes were huge in her face, searching his angular countenance for some sign of softness. But there was none. He was telling her, without any attempt to cushion it, that she was not wanted in his life. Blind panic compelled her to say, 'But I heard—you promised——'

'What?'

The words barely made it past her parched, clamped throat. 'You promised Grandad you'd look after me,' she whispered. 'I heard you.'

'And I will. As soon as his will is probated I'll invest what money there is so that you can use the interest to help you through university. I've discussed this with your godmother, and she agrees with me that this will be best for you. She's quite happy to have you stay with her until you get on your feet.'

Eden almost whimpered, her fairy castle of nascent hopes and dreams crashing in shards around her. Such pain as she had never experienced kept her silent, otherwise, she knew with a deep humiliation that was going to mark her for life, she would have pleaded and wept, begged to stay with him.

'You don't,' he went on casually, 'have to go immediately, of course. Thea's coming up in ten days' time to spend a week or so, and you can go back down with her.'

Somewhere in her abject anguish a tiny ember of pride smouldered. Eden Rogers would not be packed off from Onemahutu as though she were of no account at all.

From somewhere she summoned the pride to say as levelly as she could, 'That's kind of her, but if I'm going I might as well go as quickly as I can. Thank you.'

# CHAPTER SEVEN

IN THE end, with two cartons of goods forwarded on the carrier, Eden went down by bus a week before Thea was due to arrive. In after years she could never remember anything of the trip down; she expended so much energy keeping a calm face that nothing was left for anything else.

From somewhere she managed to scrape up the raw courage to function normally; she even smiled as she said goodbye to everyone. The fact that Blade spent most of the time away on a buying trip, and that when he was at home he was glacially remote, helped her composure too.

She hated him, hated the fact that he could so easily banish her, that his promise to her grandfather had just been lying words to soothe an old man. Eden wondered how she had ever thought she loved him. The determination she had admired was shown in its true colours as cold-blooded ruthlessness.

Auckland was big and bustling and busy, but Freda Chalfont was there to meet her, her friendly face beaming. As she kissed the older woman's cheek Eden bit back stupid, wasteful tears. No more tears, not now, not ever.

On the way home she explained a little more than she had been able to on the telephone. She said little about Blade, merely reiterating in a remote little voice that with her grandfather dead she couldn't stay at Onemahutu any longer.

'My dear, I'm so glad you've come to me.' Mrs Chalfont patted her knee as she set her opulent little car in motion. 'Your mother was the dearest friend I've ever had, you know, and I've always felt that she would worry to see you shut away up north like a princess in a tower, never meeting anyone or doing anything but try to keep Onemahutu going!'

Eden didn't feel up to answering this, so she said, 'I want to go to university, but I have no idea how much it'll cost. I've got some money that Mummy left me, but——'

'We'll find out. One of my friends is a lecturer there; she'll tell us who to contact. What do you want to study?'

'I want to do computers, and business studies,' Eden told her firmly, trying to hide the jagged edge to her voice. 'Management, and finances, and stuff like that.'

Mrs Chalfont sent her an astute, not unsympathetic glance. 'I see,' she murmured. 'Sensible girl.'

And Eden understood that her godmother knew why she wanted to study in that field. Knowledge was power. Eden had no intention of being left without either again.

In the end, it was surprisingly easy. She had the qualifications to get a place at university the following year, and the money her mother had left her would be enough to pay fees and keep her, if she lived as economically as possible.

'Here,' Mrs Chalfont announced firmly.

Eden looked at her, and then around the luxurious house in an exclusive street in Remuera. 'This,' she said, her voice wavering slightly, 'can hardly be termed living economically.'

'Oh, you'd pay the going rate for board, whatever that is. I'd like it very much if you would, Eden. We get on well together, don't we?'

Eden's smile wobbled a little. 'Yes, we do.'

'I'd love your company—the house has been so empty ever since the children left home, and it would be such fun if you stayed with me. If you ever decide that you want to live somewhere else, then that will be fine, but until then do stay, Eden.'

Eden had vowed never to rely on anyone else again, never to believe that someone would take care of her. But she saw a hint of pleading in her godmother's pretty face, and capitulated. 'Yes, of course I'd love to live with you,' she said. 'But to be fair, if you find that I start annoying you, you must feel that you can tell me to go, too.'

Mrs Chalfont gave her a quick hug. 'Yes, but I'm sure you won't,' she said cheerfully.

So Eden settled into the spare bedroom, making it hers, and to provide her with an immediate source of income her godmother helped her get a job in a very up-market gift boutique, which kept her busy, and entertained, during the days. With every ounce of will-power she possessed, Eden applied herself to learning how to live without Blade and without her grandfather, to cope with her grief for the one and the humiliation that was all she felt when she thought of Blade now.

She thought she managed quite well. At first her emotions were acute and embarrassing, lacerating her heart unbearably, but by telling herself that she was only in love with a figment of her imagination she managed to push her pain and the aching emptiness deeper into the recesses of her heart. In time, she hoped, she would never be able to find it again.

Grief for Sam was tempered by acceptance. She missed him unbearably, but he had been tired, ready to go. Sooner or later he would have seen through Blade, and that would have been another tribulation for him to bear in a life too full of them.

'And, darling, it's the way everyone wants to die, isn't it?' wise Freda Chalfont pointed out. 'Just slip into a doze in the sun—wonderful.'

A fortnight after she had arrived Eden got a letter from Blade. It was, she thought with a newly hatched cynicism, crushingly typical that her first thought when she saw the strong writing on the envelope was that he had changed his mind, her absence had made him realise that he loved her.

In fact, she sat still for several moments, unable to open it, until sheer fury at her weakness compelled her to rip it open.

He wrote remotely, as though he had never touched her, never laughed with her or kissed her, never been anything more than a distant acquaintance. As indeed, he hadn't been. She had never known the real Blade Hammond, the man who could promise an old, sick man that he would take care of his granddaughter, and then throw her out within a few weeks of the old man's death.

He hoped that she was enjoying life in Auckland. He enclosed the name and address of his solicitor, and if she needed to communicate with him he suggested she do it through him. Also enclosed was a cheque for the furniture, as he had arranged with her grandfather. He was, hers sincerely, Blade Hammond.

The paper fluttered down on to the floor. Eden put her hands to her face and wept, crying with all her heart for her love, stillborn at its tentative birth, for her childish stupidity and weakness, and for the long years that lay in front of her when she wouldn't know whether he was alive or dead.

But at least the distant, cruel letter killed any hope stone dead. She had been waiting, hoping...

Now she had to get on with her life.

Christmas with Mrs Chalfont and her two married sons and their families was fun, although sometimes she had to pretend to enjoy the laughter and the teasing. To her surprise they all accepted her presence without comment, welcoming her into the family with the same uncomplicated openness that characterised her godmother.

During the New Year Freda began to introduce her to a wide variety of people. Many of the older ones began their conversations with things like, 'I remember your family so well. We used to stay at Onemahutu...'

The house parties and entertainments had started to dwindle before she was ten, but it was clear that her grandparents' talent for hospitality was a fond memory in the hearts of many people. Eden listened to these reminiscences with a rather painful pride.

Slowly she began to put names to faces, to form tentative friendships with others of her own age, no longer protesting when Freda suggested she go with her to various functions. It helped that so many people knew her name, and after a short period of self-consciousness she gained enough confidence to enjoy herself.

One night, at a party rather more elaborate than any she had been to, she was accosted by a woman of about twenty-six or seven, a glittery, glamorous creature in a dress that as well as being shamelessly seductive must have cost a small fortune.

'You're Eden Rogers, aren't you?' the stranger asked with a carelessness belied by her expression. 'From Onemahutu in Northland?'

Eden confirmed that, yes, she was Eden Rogers.

'I'm Andrea Sinclair. Tell me, is it true that you've been living with Blade Hammond?'

Eden's head lifted. She cringed inside, especially as she realised that others about them were watching and listening.

'I lived with my grandfather in the same house,' she returned, pronouncing each word with crisp precision.

The other woman's shoulder hunched. 'Oh, well, you know what I mean,' she said pettishly. 'How is he? Blade, I mean.'

'As far as I know he's fine.' Eden's voice was steady, she was relieved to hear.

There was something unsettling in Andrea Sinclair's expression, something avid and greedy. 'Did he tell you how he got the money to buy your place?' she asked, dropping her voice a little.

Repelled, Eden shook her head. 'It's none of my business.' Or yours, her tone implied.

Hard colour mantled the other woman's cheeks. 'He got that money by making love to me and then accepting a small fortune from my father not to marry me,' she said, lifting her voice as though she wanted to be heard.

Eden's heart stopped. 'What?'

'You heard. Oh, he's wonderful, isn't he? A magnificent animal, an even more magnificent lover, but his sexuality is very firmly controlled by his greed, believe me. His mother worked for my father, and Blade decided he wanted that sort of good life for himself, so he cast around to get it, and this was the easiest way. How else do you think he got enough money scraped together to buy a station, even a run-down old place like yours? Not through hard work, believe me.'

Eden flinched, horribly aware that there was now a little pool of silence all around them. She couldn't think of anything to say to this wholly embarrassing woman with her vile accusations and her general air of unbalance.

However, the opportunity to soothe her was lost. Andrea Sinclair resumed with a nasty hint of innuendo, 'He enjoyed every moment of the lovemaking, mind you, but once he got the money he dumped me without ceremony.'

Eden felt sick. She looked into feral blue eyes, and said gently, 'I'm sorry if that's what he did, but it's really no concern of mine——'

And was given a desperate smile, filled with seasoned malice. 'Perhaps not, but, once everyone knows what he did, he's not going to be welcome in any decent person's house, even if he did buy Onemahutu,' the older woman said in a malevolently lowered voice. 'And that's what he wants, you know. He's a social climber of the worst sort.'

Eden found this impossible to believe. Blade didn't need to crash society; he possessed an effortless charisma that would ensure him a place in any level of society he wanted to move in.

'You don't believe me.' Andrea's eyes narrowed as they searched Eden's face. 'He hated being the housekeeper's bastard son,' she went on softly. 'He hated being nobody. He's jealous, and greedy and clever. My father was a bloody-minded old snob, but he was clever. He told Blade he'd cut me off without a penny if we married, and then offered him a pay-off. Blade was more than happy to take it.'

There was something febrile, some driven note in the woman's voice that made the hairs stand up on the back of Eden's neck. She said quickly, 'Miss Sinclair, I doubt very much whether I'll see Blade again——'

'Oh, you might.' The other woman's blue eyes drifted down over Eden's face. 'If he can't find a rich, well-connected, *obedient* woman to marry, he might come back to you. After all, you've got the connections and the style, even though you haven't got a penny. And you look as though you might turn into the maternal type when you grow up. Blade Hammond's an ambitious man; he plans ahead. He wants to start a dynasty, and he wants his children to have the background he hasn't got. He doesn't care how he gets what he wants. Just remember that, if he comes sniffing around.'

She turned and disappeared into the swirl of people, and she must have left Auckland soon after, for Eden didn't see her again.

But the shocking story she had imparted stayed buried deep in Eden's heart like a seeping poison.

At first university was huge and intimidating, but as she became accustomed to it she became more confident. However, she had been there for over six months before she felt secure enough to accept an invitation from a man. The first time it was with a trepidation she knew her godmother shared, but somewhat to her surprise she found herself enjoying the evening.

She panicked a bit when he kissed her, but that was all he did, and she enjoyed that too. No bells went off, but she hadn't expected any. Familiarity, she told herself as she accepted another invitation, would soon stop her comparing every man to Blade.

So she found her place, revelling in her work at university, enjoying the social life there and in her godmother's circle, making friends cautiously because that was her nature. At the end of the first year she surprised herself by doing extremely well in her examinations.

With her results came the surprising realisation that she was no longer in love with Blade Hammond. She hardly ever thought of him now, except when he appeared in the newspaper, which he did more and more often. He was beginning to be called upon as a spokesman for primary producers, and once one of the daily papers devoted its whole agricultural section to him, detailing what he was doing on Onemahutu. It was eulogistic in manner; Eden read it carefully, and when she had finished she stared for a long moment at the photograph of Blade that accompanied it, tall and strong and lithe, his dog at his side.

He looked the same, she thought dispassionately, the strong face and intensely masculine beauty hiding the real man. And he was certainly achieving the success he had planned with Sam. Onemahutu was becoming a show-piece. The journalist said nothing about a wife, so presumably Blade and Thea were still conducting their long-distance affair.

Eden cut the article out and put it in her bottom drawer. Her heart, she thought proudly, didn't even thump.

Halfway through her second year away from Onemahutu she met Iain Stephenson at a dinner party, and liked him immediately. He was big and fair and—solid, she thought, except that 'solid' sounded wrong. Dependable, perhaps? Laughing blue eyes and a rakish smile couldn't hide the rock-bottom integrity of the man.

When he asked her out she accepted, and within a month it was accepted that they were a duo, invited everywhere together. As the year wound down Eden found herself wondering why she didn't desire Iain. He was patently in love with her, and she loved him in return, she respected him, she liked his warm mouth and the soft slide of his hands over her skin.

But light caresses were all she could bear. When his hands began to tremble and his kisses deepened, she pulled back, worried, angry, sick at heart because it seemed that Blade still cast a dark shadow over her even from this distance. Why, when she had responded with mindless ardour to *his* kisses, *his* touch, couldn't she find the same magic in Iain's touch?

Finally, just before Christmas, she told him that she could not see him again.

'I love you,' he said, his pleasant face rigid.

She winced, lifting great smudged eyes. 'I love you, too, but it's not the sort of love you want, or deserve,' she insisted painfully.

'I suppose I always knew.' His mouth twisted. 'I'm not going to try to persuade you because I can't think of anything more suicidal than marrying a woman who can't bear me to touch her, but perhaps you'd better find the man who built the barricades you hide behind.'

'There's no one.'

He bent and kissed her very lightly. 'Yes, there is. Face it, Eden, and do something about it, unless you want to ache for his touch for the rest of your life.'

She missed Iain. She had come to depend on him, to love him. With him she had felt safe. It was another thing to blame Blade for, that she couldn't let the man she loved make love to her.

What had Blade done to her? Imprinted her, the way a chicken was imprinted by the first thing it saw after hatching?

That summer she worked for a friend of Freda's, gaining practical experience in an office, and enjoying it. Her employer was pleased with her, too, to the extent of offering her a job after she had finished her degree. Eden thanked him prettily, but for some reason avoided giving a straight acceptance.

The following year was one of solid work. Her papers stimulated her and stretched her brain, so she had little time for a social life. Iain had moved down to Wellington, where he was now working for the Department of Internal Affairs. Eden still missed him, but honesty compelled her to admit that she missed his laughter and his companionship far more than she missed his caresses. Perhaps she had wanted the security of being loved by him. Slowly it was being borne in upon her that the only security she could rely on was in herself.

By the end of November she knew that she had graduated well, and that from now on she was in charge of her life.

'Wonderful!' Mrs Chalfont exulted, as pleased as if it were her own child. 'We're going to have a celebration, and then you, dearest, are going to loaf! Your thin little face is even thinner, your cheekbones are too prominent, and those pretty eyes have great dark circles under them. We'll go up to Kawau Island and stay at the bach over Christmas.'

Eden was only just realising how tired she was, and the prospect of long, lazy days by the sea beckoned alluringly. Her CV was out to every organisation she hoped might be interested, but of course no one was hiring just before Christmas. They had all promised to contact her when the offices opened again in the middle of January.

'I won't know myself,' she said, yawning. 'It sounds heavenly. Nothing to do but lie around in the sun. Suitably slathered in sun-block, of course.'

'You've done precious little relaxing for the past three years.' Freda smiled affectionately. 'But now you've got where you wanted to, and so I decree that for one summer you do absolutely nothing but wallow in sybaritic idleness. Of course there'll be all the end-of-year parties here for you to enjoy, but summer in Kawau is perfect— long, hot days and warm nights, sailing, swimming, barbecues...'

'Bliss,' Eden said sleepily, wriggling her slender body around in the hammock slung from two strong branches of the jacaranda tree. One long, slender hand drooped limply over the side.

Freda smiled. 'It will be. You're confident enough to enjoy it now, without wondering whether you're going to make a *faux pas* and end up with your foot in your mouth.'

Eden's soft laughter held a rueful note. 'Was it so obvious? Yes, I suppose it was. Green as grass, wasn't I?'

'You were such an innocent little soul, yet you had the determination to overcome that massive crush you were suffering from, put the man completely from your mind and really set yourself to making something of your life. I was proud of you, and your mother would have been too.'

Heat ebbed from Eden's skin, then flowed back in. 'I must have been like an open book,' she sighed.

'No, not entirely. In fact you kept your emotions under very tight control. Certainly you were young for your age in some ways. In others you were much older, far more disciplined, but emotionally you were a baby. You've grown up, Eden, since then.'

If he saw her now, would Blade notice?

The stray thought emerged from her unconscious with the lethal aim of a bullet. She turned away from her godmother's altogether too astute gaze, embarrassed that after three long years she could still care what Blade Hammond thought of her.

She faked a yawn, hoping that Mrs Chalfont would think that was why her voice was odd. 'Are you going to the Hornings' party?' she murmured.

'Yes. Coming?'

'Mmm.'

'Wear your pretty lemon dress,' Mrs Chalfont advised. 'I love the way it turns your eyes to topazes.'

'Ah, but you love cats.'

The older woman smiled. 'True, but it's an excellent cut for you.'

'You mean,' grumbled Eden, 'that it makes me look a little more voluptuous in the bust region.'

'Well, yes, although you have a very fashionable figure. You're too self-conscious about your supposed lack there.'

'I suppose I am,' Eden said slowly. Until she had envied Thea her superb breasts she had accepted her physical deficiencies with wry resignation.

Common sense told her that she couldn't blame Blade for all of the things that had gone wrong in her life, but sometimes, she thought with grim amusement, he came in very handy!

Fleur and Jasper Horning were a pleasant couple, both doctors, both youngish and modern and fun, and their parties were always good. This one took place in the back yard of their old villa in Herne Bay around a very up-market pool and barbecue area, heavily scented by datura flowers that glimmered like cool white trumpets in the dusk.

Eden was now completely at home in such surroundings. With a glass of champagne in her hand, she talked and laughed and greeted friends with a sparkling assurance that drew accustomed attention. She had learned how to make-up to accentuate the green in her eyes, and the soft tenderness of her mouth, wisely not powdering her superb skin.

Shadowy eyes gleaming with pleasure in her oval face, she mingled with the other guests, a vibrant butterfly in her lemon silk dress. Fleur and Jasper had a wide-ranging group of friends and acquaintances, so you never knew who was going to be at their parties; Eden met a world-famous yachtsman, a financier who was supposed to be the up-and-coming man, a writer whose last book everyone knew to be a masterpiece, although no one had understood it, and the latest model sensation, her crowning glory of blue-black hair all that could be discerned through the press of men surrounding her.

Eden was having fun. Until she came around the side of a trellis and walked through an archway smothered in climbing roses—straight into Blade Hammond.

It was like hitting a wall—hard, solid, immovable, but no wall was warm, and no wall possessed that faint, erotic scent of sun and salt and potent male, the scent she had come to realise was his alone. And no wall had ever looked down at her with raised brows and eyes that were as blue as winter skies, clear and cool and enigmatic.

No other man had the power to send the blood rioting through her body, touching off signals all the way from the top of her head to her curling toes in their high-heeled sandals.

'Oops!' she said intelligently, staggering backwards, so appalled that she quite literally couldn't think of anything to say.

He had grabbed her by the arm, and was now holding her upright, the strength that had always intimidated her very much to the fore.

'I'm afraid your champagne got spilt,' he said pleasantly, as though they had seen each other only a few minutes before. 'I'll get you another.'

'No, don't bother; it's my second glass, and I only ever drink one.' The words sounded all right, almost as though she knew what she was saying. Eden drew a deep breath and stepped out of his grasp, dragging her eyes away from that hard, handsome face. 'I've had enough,' she managed, and even summoned a smile to go with the words, careless and casual, as though her heart weren't beating like a runaway metronome in her throat.

He took the glass from her shaking fingers and tucked it into the stems of the rose. Casually he turned her around and, with his hand firm at her elbow, propelled her back into the dimly lit garden, where the scent of the datura blossoms pervaded the air and the hubbub of the party died into a low mutter.

By the time she realised what he was doing, and that she didn't want to be there with him, he had sat her down on a rustic seat beneath an arbour of jasmine, and was standing beside her like a warder, she thought waspishly, trying with all her will-power to calm her shattered nerves with a healthy dose of common sense.

'How are you?' he asked calmly, his hooded gaze fixed on her slightly averted profile in a distinctly unnerving way.

'Fine.' Two could play this game. 'And you?'

'Well enough.' There was a flash of white that indicated a smile—a rather wolfish one, she thought, as her eyes became more attuned to the darkness.

'I hear you're doing great things at Onemahutu,' she said in her best social manner, her composure slowly recovering as she realised she wasn't breaking apart in front of him.

'I hear you're doing great things down here.' His voice was bland, but there was an undertone of sardonic amusement that brought her chin up fractionally.

'Really?' She infused her tone with delicate sarcasm.

He smiled again, and, yes, it definitely was not a tame sort of smile; it had distinctly feral overtones. 'Yes,' he said simply.

This, she decided, with a flash of sheer anger, could go on all night, and she hadn't come here so that he could enjoy himself making her look a fool.

'I didn't realise that my fame had extended as far north as Onemahutu, but I'm going to graduate with A's,' she told him calmly. 'I'm certainly pleased with my results.'

'I imagine you must be.' He sounded quietly amused. 'So what are you planning to do now?'

'I don't really know. I've sent my CV around, but I might, perhaps, go on and do a Master's.'

'On the other hand...?'

Oh, he'd always been astute. 'On the other hand, I'm bored with lectures. I want to do something real.' She shrugged. 'Perhaps it's because I'm older than many of the other graduates.'

'What are your options?'

She told him, and for a while they discussed some directions she could take in her career, just like distant acquaintances. Except that acquaintances didn't give her this pounding, skipping pulse and such suddenly sharpened perceptions, so that she thought she could see straight through the thickening darkness, become permeated with the erotic scent of the trumpet flowers and the jasmine, feel small shivery impulses through her skin right down to her bones, impulses of electricity that emanated from Blade.

Unfortunately the physical magic was still as strong, as unmanageable as ever. No other man had ever managed to raise the slightest bit of response in her. What if Blade Hammond, a man who was totally lacking in any sort of honour, was the only man who could?

Unable to deal then and there with that horrifying supposition, Eden suppressed her fears and conversed, she hoped, with composure and a certain amount of intelligence, until there came one of those natural pauses in any conversation, a pause she filled with a smooth query as to how he happened to be at the Hornings' party.

'Jasper's an old friend,' he replied, 'and when he realised that I was down here on business he suggested I come along.'

A tiny hope expired, so well-concealed that she hadn't even realised its existence until it died. Of course he hadn't come looking for her! Colour faded from her skin, leaving her cold and clammy.

'They're a nice couple,' she said vaguely, barely able to breathe because of the pain. She got up. 'I'd better get back to the party.'

He didn't protest, but merely smiled and went with her. Bitterly, she thought that he was the only man she had ever felt so—so *safe* with. Perhaps that was why she was addicted to him. Perhaps she was a wimp, looking for a strong man to take the responsibility for her happiness, her life, on his broad shoulders. Her mouth twisted sardonically. No, that wasn't so, otherwise she'd have married Iain. But she was going to have to find out why Blade, and only Blade, had this awful debilitating effect on her independence.

And her mind, and her heart.

Once back in the crowded environs of the party area, she was able to slip away after a few minutes, although she wondered bleakly whether it would have been so easy if he'd wanted her to stay beside him.

Desperation widened her eyes, turning them glittery. Freda was enjoying herself too much to go home now, and, anyway, Eden was damned if she was going to run away. So she forced herself to laugh and flirt and appear

to have a good time, while everywhere she looked it
seemed she saw Blade, tall, his hair gleaming amber in
the lights, overpoweringly charismatic, that in-built sensuality leashed yet blatantly compelling.

Soon, she promised herself with gritted teeth, she was
going to work out exactly what he did to her and how,
and then she was going to exorcise him from her life. It
was degrading to be so enslaved by a physical passion.

The beginnings of a headache throbbed silently at one
temple. She sat down in the dense shade of a magnolia
tree with a glass of soda water, sipping it slowly, trying
to stave off the pain. The lights blurred and swung,
melding the bright dresses of the women into a kal-
eidoscope of hues, rich and bright and pretty against the
warm darkness and the glowing green waters of the pool.

Without volition she searched the crowd until her gaze
came to rest on hair the colour of manuka honey, a
striking, arrogant profile, a mouth as splendidly sculpted
as some pagan statue of old. He was listening with un-
smiling concentration to the financier, nodding slightly
as the other man spoke. He looked tough, and powerful,
and ruthless—a man anyone could be forgiven for fearing
a little.

Yet Eden was not afraid of him. She hated the effect
he had on her, but she didn't fear him. And there was
no deceit, no deliberate cruelty in the hard-planed angles
of his face.

Where had she seen hair that exact shade before? Eyes
half closed, her soft mouth held in a disciplined line,
Eden pondered, until suddenly it came to her. The
woman who had told her that Blade had seduced her,
then accepted a pay-off not to marry her—Andrea
Sinclair, that was her name.

How odd that she should share that unusual hair
colour with the man she had been betrayed by!

She had forgotten completely about the woman and
her sordid little story. Or had she pushed it so far into
her subconscious that it needed the unexpected sight of
Blade to bring it back?

Except that Eden had never been quite able to convince herself that the Sinclair woman had told the truth. She had pretended to believe her because at that time it had suited her purposes to do so; she'd needed all the defences she could muster against Blade. But deep in her heart she had known that, whatever had happened, Blade would not have allowed a man to pay him off. Ambitious he certainly was, but he was prepared to work for his aims. Seducing a woman and then blackmailing her father was simply not the way he worked. It was a kind of sexual opportunism she couldn't imagine him indulging in.

Oh, come off it! she scoffed, lifting the glass to her mouth with a trembling hand. You know what he did to you! Promised your grandfather to look after you, and then threw you out! After coaxing your grandfather to lend him your money for at least six years. Surely Andrea Sinclair, in spite of her febrile spite and malice, had been telling the truth?

The truth was, Eden concluded, she was so besotted by the man that she was still trying her best to make excuses for him.

And that was dangerous.

Oh, why did he have to turn up now, just when she was getting her life together?

He laughed suddenly, and then looked across the crowd as though he could see her in the dark. Eden shrank back, but he nodded and left the financier, working his way across the crowd, not hurrying, yet moving with the deliberate grace she had been so powerfully attracted to ever since she had first seen him.

'What's the matter?' he asked as he came into the peaceful darkness.

She parried, 'Does anything have to be the matter?'

'I think so. You're not in the habit of hiding yourself away any more, are you?'

'No.' He took the glass from her hand and pulled her to her feet with a cool, imperative grip as she sighed, 'I'm in the throes of getting a headache.'

'I'll take you home.'

Her eyes moved to where Mrs Chalfont was laughing with a group of old friends.

'No,' she countered calmly, 'I'll get a taxi.'

'I'm going now anyway, and you might as well come with me. It's not very far out of my way to take you home. If you like I'll go and tell your godmother that you're a little off-colour.'

She should have said no, but she was weak. 'All right.'

He was driving a big BMW, a powerful thing that whispered along the motorway. Onemahutu was definitely paying its way now, Eden thought snidely as she pulled the soft lemon silk of her skirt over her slim legs. She allowed herself a small look at his hands on the wheel, relaxed, long-fingered, totally competent, then snatched her gaze away. Blade belonged to the past—if only he'd stayed there, instead of intruding into the present!

Deliberately she began to breathe slowly and easily, seeking to control the wildfire temptation coursing through her body with techniques Freda had taught her. Normally they worked; this time she was unable to dampen her nervous exhilaration entirely.

He didn't ask her where she lived, but of course he knew. Their solicitors communicated with each other once a year or so. When the car drew up outside she said quietly, 'Thank you.'

Goodbye, her heart said.

He lifted his brows, but made no reply, not even when he took the key from her fingers and opened the door.

'Thank you,' Eden said again, this time a little more crisply.

He slanted her a taunting smile and went in with her to Freda's pretty drawing-room, looking around him with evident interest. He should have been out of place in such a feminine room, but he dominated it with the natural authority that stamped itself on any surroundings.

'You'd better get off to bed,' he told her, enigmatic blue eyes finally coming to rest on her strained face.

She nodded. 'Yes, all right.'

He touched her cheek, his gaze suddenly sharp. 'And when you're thinking clearly you need to decide what to do with the furniture and stuff you left at Onemahutu,' he said.

Dazedly she shook her head. 'What furniture?'

'Everything in the house is yours. I've not done anything about it while you were at university because you had no place to put it, but you'll have to make up your mind now.'

'I thought you bought it. You sent a cheque—a lot of money—after I left, and said it was for the furniture.' The words stumbled out.

'That was for its hire,' he explained blandly. 'Let me know what you want done with it.' He bent and kissed her cheek. 'Goodnight, Eden. You've grown up very nicely.'

'If that's so,' she blurted, driven by some unknown compulsion, 'does that mean that I can have the money Grandad left me now?'

His eyes gleamed with an ironic challenge. 'Why don't you come up to Onemahutu so that I can see whether you really have, or whether that elegant little air of sophistication is just surface polish?'

After the soft growl of the big car had died away Eden went up to her bedroom, aware in some dim part of her mind that the headache had gone completely. Tension, she told herself.

And then, Oh, God, it's starting all over again!

She lay awake until the dawn came, her mind racing around like a mouse in a maze. But as the summer sun came leaping over the horizon, irradiating a hushed, dew-wet world, she came to the reluctant, weary conclusion that she was going to have to go up to Onemahutu. She needed to know what sort of man Blade was; surely, now that she had grown up, she would be able to discern whether he was as ruthless as his actions seemed to indicate, or whether there were reasons she didn't know for his behaviour?

And somehow she had to get this degrading passion out of her system. Absence hadn't been able to do it, so perhaps familiarity might do the trick...

Eden woke with her mind made up, but she had no intention of going back to Onemahutu until after the New Year. Let him see, she decided, that she was not easily manipulated. So she had her time on Kawau, soaking up the lazy, beach ambience, and spent a hilarious Christmas with the people she now considered her family.

Ten edgy days later she rang up. The telephone buzzed until she was certain no one was there, but, just as she was ready to put the receiver down, Blade's voice, cool and uncommunicative, came on. 'Hello.'

Biting her lip, she hesitated. Was she doing the right thing? Should she refuse to have anything more to do with him, and communicate only through lawyers? She didn't really need the legacy—she could keep herself as soon as she got a job—but the seductive need to prove to him that she had matured, that she was no longer the child who had fallen head over heels in love with him, was as strong as caution.

'Who's there?' he asked, a silky warning note underlining the words.

'Eden. I'm coming up by bus tomorrow,' she said, trying to sound as confident as he did. 'Can somebody pick me up from the end of the road?'

'I'll be in town tomorrow; I'll collect you from the depot.' There was nothing to be gained from his voice.

'All right,' she agreed evenly. 'I'll see you then.'

It was raining when she left Warkworth the next morning, but it soon cleared, and after Whangarei she was able to look out with interested eyes. Observing the differences the last three years had made to the landscape took her mind off her thoughts, and helped stabilise the uncomfortable lurch in her stomach. Lord, she hoped she was doing the right thing!

She certainly didn't get any reassurance from Blade. The sun was shining with that special northern heat when she got out of the bus, and he was waiting in the shade of the shop veranda, casually dressed, as much at home on the wide street as he had been in Freda Chalfont's elegant drawing-room.

'Hi,' Eden said, determined not to be nervous although bubbles far more potent than those of champagne were fizzing through her bloodstream.

'Hello.' He smiled down at her as though she was the only person he saw. 'Is that all your luggage?'

'There's a case in the freight compartment.'

It wasn't very big, and he hefted it without any difficulty. 'Come on,' he said, leading the way to the Land Rover.

'What happened to the BMW?'

His teeth showed in a smile. 'I flew down that weekend. It was a hire car.'

So much for her sneering thoughts, but she couldn't keep a snap out of her voice when she asked, 'Trying to impress someone? Thea, perhaps?' Or Thea's successor.

'No.' Well, no, of course not. Blade didn't *try* to impress; it just came naturally. He certainly didn't need expensive cars to do it. 'I need a big car to fit my legs in,' he explained calmly. 'Onemahutu is doing well, but there's not money for big cars yet.'

'I see.' She didn't really want to know how he was doing for money—unless he was indicating that he had no intention of releasing hers.

'And Thea is married,' he continued with a fine thread of mockery in the deep, even voice. 'She lives in Wellington, and has a small daughter, and, I believe, another baby due in three months or so.'

Which seemed to dispose of Thea. A tiny sore patch in Eden's heart was miraculously eased.

'How long do you intend to stay?' he asked, a little abruptly, as he eased the vehicle out on to the road, and set off for Onemahutu.

Noticing that her hands were twisting uneasily together in her lap, Eden deliberately stilled the long, tanned fingers. 'Not very long,' she said composedly.

'Longing for the bright lights already?' He didn't attempt to hide the derisive note in his voice.

She shrugged, determined not to be goaded. 'I have to be back in Auckland when the firms start opening their doors, in case any of them want to employ me.'

'Then shall we give it a fortnight?'

'OK.' Her voice was light, casual, as though it meant nothing to her. As it didn't, of course. She was up here to get him out of her system; that was all. 'Tell me about Onemahutu. Is Paul still there? And Abe and Maria Rawhiri?'

'Yes. Paul has more or less retired, which means that he works as hard, but protests when he's paid for it. Abe and Maria have just got their first grandchild, and are over the moon about it.'

Relaxing insensibly, she smiled with genuine pleasure. She had forgotten how deep and attractive his voice was, how much she liked the sound of it. 'I'll just bet they are! I've read the occasional article about the situation,' she murmured. 'Everything seems to be going well.'

He slanted her a swift glance. 'We've had three good years. Are you trying to delicately enquire whether I have Sam's legacy intact?'

'No.' She looked directly at him, her mouth tight with anger. 'But, as you've brought the subject up, have you?'

'Yes,' he said calmly. 'It's been invested these past three years in stocks and bonds.'

'Oh. I wondered——' She stopped, aware of just how crass her suspicions would seem. .

But Blade was smiling. 'You wondered whether I was using your money to help get the station back on its feet,' he finished for her gently.

Her skin pulled tight in the age-old instinctive recognition of danger, but she retorted, 'Yes.'

'I had enough money to buy the station and get it back on to its feet,' he said calmly, 'enough to keep it running for two years. If I hadn't had the money, I'd have bought a smaller, cheaper property. I haven't spent anything on luxuries, but I'm not so poor that I'd think of robbing you of your few thousand dollars. Besides, if I'd used your money, that would have given you some claim on Onemahutu. And I definitely didn't want that.' His tone cut like a whip, contemptuous, filled with cold and controlled menace.

Colour fled Eden's cheeks, then washed back. 'I'm not accusing you——' she began awkwardly, but that icy tone interrupted before she could go any further.

'It sounded like it to me. Do you really believe that I would cheat you, Eden?'

'Well, you never gave me any reason to believe anything else,' she rounded on him, her voice deep and huskily furious, her eyes snapping with fury. 'You told Grandad that you'd look after me, and then you threw me out as soon as you could——'

'There hasn't been a week that I haven't heard from Freda Chalfont,' he retorted curtly, swinging the car off the highway on to the narrow metal road. Instantly a cloud of white dust boiled after them, cutting them off from all behind them.

# CHAPTER EIGHT

EDEN stared at Blade's inflexible profile, warily noting the signs of temper in his expression. 'I don't believe you,' she said slowly, harshly. 'Why would you do that?'

Instead of carrying on up the road, he drove into the metal dump. Eden's mouth dried suddenly, but he was silent until they were hidden from passers-by behind the weeping willow tree Tod had chosen to park under the night he had taken her to the Harveys' party. Now she couldn't even remember Tod's face.

Blade leaned back in the seat, hands still clasping the wheel. His mouth curved into a smile that paradoxically made her shrink away. 'Why do you think I'd keep in such close touch with her?'

'I don't know.' Her voice was thin and wild. She felt sick, as though the carefully constructed edifice of her emotions and beliefs was crumbling before her eyes, revealed to be nothing more than a chimera.

'When you were fourteen,' he began calmly, once more fully in control of himself, 'I promised myself that I'd marry somebody like you. You had style, the promise of great beauty, excellent breeding. But you were fourteen. I came back to Onemahutu,' he said between his teeth, 'to see whether you were still available.'

Eden closed her eyes, sickened by his calculation, the cold-blooded, methodical, unwavering determination that had kept him on this path, ignoring her needs, her emotions.

'Then why did you throw me out?' she asked tonelessly. 'God knows, it must have been patently obvious that I was fathoms deep in love with you.'

'I couldn't marry a child, and that's all you were.'

She flinched. 'You were cruel.'

172

'Hell,' he swore, the fury in his tone jerking her lashes up, 'I drove you away because my baser self was urging me to take you while I could, to bind you to me with every tie there is—sexual, legal, emotional—and I knew that, if I did that, I'd take everything you needed from you!'

'I needed you!'

'No, you didn't; you needed to grow up, to go out into the world and find your own way—you needed to discover that you were capable of independence.' His big hands clenched on the wheel until the knuckles turned white. 'I had to let you go. I wanted you so much I could taste the wanting and the need, harsh and bitter in my mouth!'

'I don't believe it,' she said, truly shocked, her great, smudged eyes searching the hard outline of his face.

He showed his teeth in a smile that had no humour, only a dreadful irony. 'It's the truth. I think it started when you used to come down to the wool-shed to watch me shear. I was touched by the fact that you had a crush on me—you were so sweet, so shy, like a small fawn with your wide green-brown eyes and your long, thin little arms and legs, small and slender... Yet you also had courage and heart and sweetness, and a patrician little air that I liked. I used to look forward to seeing you every day, to see you smile. And a couple of times it occurred to me that in six or seven years you'd make the sort of wife I was looking for.'

She said uncertainly, 'You sound so cold-blooded about it.'

'If I was, I've been punished for it.' Staring ahead, he gave a brief, mirthless smile. 'Then, three years ago, I heard through the grapevine that you were working Onemahutu. I thought I'd see what sort of woman you'd grown into.' He looked down at his hands as though they were unfamiliar to him, and, with an effort that was palpable, relaxed them. But there was a note of bitter black frustration in his voice as he went on, 'But you were exactly the same—as though for five years you'd existed in a time warp. Still that heartbreakingly innocent, exquisite child.'

In the years she had been away Eden had been told often enough that she was lovely, that she was pretty, that she was attractive and chic and stylish and—oh, the synonyms were common enough! But no one had ever told her she was exquisite.

That it should be Blade who said so took her breath away. She said uncertainly, 'I—you behaved like a kind big brother.'

'All I felt at first was affection with a touch of lust. I looked you over, looked Onemahutu over, and decided that I'd buy the one and marry the other. It was time I married, and for reasons of my own I wanted a wife who had the qualities you possessed. That you were completely innocent would merely make my task easier. And I hadn't been there more than a couple of days when I saw that your grandfather was worrying himself sick about what was going to happen to you. I had a pretty good idea he'd be happy enough to see you married to me.'

'So you bought Onemahutu.' Eden's voice was harsh, almost ragged, her heart breaking. 'What put you off the marriage?'

'When I kissed you after the top-dressing crash, I realised that you were completely, totally unawakened. By then I knew that once I had you I was never going to be able to let you go.' He spoke slowly, hard, cold determination giving his voice a wintry note. 'How could I trap you like that, by locking you into marriage before you had any knowledge of your own needs and desires? And then,' he said heavily, 'there was Tod Blair.'

She made a muffled sound, and he nodded. 'Exactly. I knew after that night that you had to go.'

'Why?' It was beginning to make some sense now; she was at last able to discern some sort of pattern behind the shifts of attitude that had so bewildered her three years ago.

'It was a big enough set-back when I kissed you that first time and clearly terrified you with the very mild caress I gave you. But I stupidly let you persuade me into sharing your bed,' he said dispassionately. 'I spent all night suffering from frustration, and you slept like a child in my arms. I had to keep my mind off the fact that you were slim and sweet and seductively curved, that I wanted you more than I had ever wanted any other woman, by imagining the worst sorts of punishments for the little oaf, and you snuggled against me as though I were your mother!'

He showed his teeth. 'It so patently meant absolutely nothing to you. Then the next morning you thanked me with clear, transparent sincerity for comforting you, when it had been all I could do to stop myself ripping off that nightgown and burying myself in you to ease the hunger I'd let grow to almost unmanageable proportions.'

Eden understood now.

'Yes,' he continued, those clear eyes blazing with sapphire fire as they rested on her astonished face, 'you had to go, so that you could grow up, and discover for yourself what *you* wanted, what was right for *you*. All your life people had made decisions for you. You needed to learn how to make them for yourself.'

'So you made the final one, and sent me away.'

He said bleakly, 'It was the only thing I could do for you. I told you once that my mother was a housekeeper on a high-country station. What I didn't tell you was that my father was her employer.' He was still looking ahead, so he didn't see her eyes widen and then narrow as she struggled with this new knowledge.

In a monotone he went on, 'She was vulnerable. I don't know what sort of relationship they had, as they were discreet—I never saw any signs of affection between them, and I was almost ten when I found out that he was my father. He was married, you see, and his wife discovered it somehow; I wandered in on the aftermath.'

Eden's heart was wrung. She put her hand on Blade's arm, feeling the moment of shock, that physical reaction that was like a lightning strike, and then the rigid muscles. He hated telling her this.

'Whatever, he took advantage of her,' he said harshly. A muscle flicked against his jawbone, emphasising the white line around his compressed mouth. 'He never recognised me while he was alive, but he left me money in his will. With that and my savings I had enough to buy Onemahutu. But I was not going to see you in the same vulnerable position, almost forced by circumstances to marry me.'

'I met Andrea Sinclair,' Eden told him baldly. 'About a month after I left Onemahutu.'

'My beautiful half-sister.' His mouth curved into a smile that stopped her heart in her throat. 'A bitch, isn't she? She was trained from childhood to hate me, of course.'

'I didn't know she was your half-sister, and she didn't tell me. Quite the opposite, in fact.'

'What *did* she tell you?'

Eden was beginning to regret that she had mentioned the other woman, but, if the vicious Andrea was going about spreading her disgusting rumours, he should know. 'She said that you had made love to her, and that the money you used to buy Onemahutu was money her father paid you off with. She said that you were a social climber—desperate, she supposed, to make up for the fact that you were a bastard. What she was trying to do was blacken your name so well that no one of any importance would invite you into their house.'

'And you believed her, of course.' Blade's voice was level, almost uninterested, but Eden did not make the mistake of thinking it revealed a lack of emotion. She was learning to read him, this man she loved, and to understand that he hid his emotions because he had been taught that it was dangerous to reveal them.

She hesitated. 'I didn't know——'

He was merciless. 'You believed her.'

Stiffly, she retorted, 'No. Oh, I tried; it seemed to me that it was just the sort of thing I could imagine you doing, but—I'm a bastard too. It certainly hasn't turned me into a social climber or a blackmailer. And in my heart I knew you wouldn't behave like that.'

'Even though I reneged on my promise to your grandfather?'

She directed a long, steady look his way, seeing the masterful strength that was the outward manifestation of his character. 'But you didn't, did you?' There was silence, neither agreeing nor dissenting, then she said, 'So you invited Thea up.'

'Yes. We weren't lovers then, although we had been. Thea's a realist; she knew she'd never be happy in the country, so by the time she arrived at Onemahutu we were just good friends. She knew what she was there for, however, and threw herself a little too enthusiastically into acting the part of lover.'

She had been clever, too. Eden's mouth tightened. Before she could speak he went on, 'But then your grandfather died, and I didn't know what to do. In the end I conspired with Freda Chalfont, who agreed wholeheartedly that you needed to get away, and that you wouldn't go of your own accord. So I threw you out.'

'Why did you challenge me to come back?' Eden still didn't know what he felt for her. Wanting was not loving. For all she knew, he'd got over that inconvenient passion, too.

Of course she loved him, had loved him all the time she had been away. That was why, fond though she was of him, Iain had never touched her innermost heart.

'Don't you know?' Blade was watching her with the cool, deliberate lack of emotion she had never forgotten.

'No.'

'Perhaps I wanted you to see that Onemahutu is in good hands.' He switched the engine on and drove through the long green fronds of the willow, his lean hands skilful and competent on the wheel.

He was right; it was in good hands. As Eden pondered his revelations, she looked around her with a knowledgeable eye. Onemahutu looked rich and loved, the pastures green and smooth, shelter-belts and woodlots dotting the rolling hills. Eroding gullies had been fenced and allowed to regenerate with native bush, and the fences and gates were in immaculate condition, as were the buildings, and the stock.

It was as she remembered it from the good days, although there were houses in places where there had never been before, and blocks of orchard, and, on the fertile bottomlands, great fields of maize. Pretty golden Jersey cows indicated the dairy farm, and there were deer, even more graceful, behind their high netting fences. Clearly Blade had managed to carry out many of his ideas; Onemahutu was much more intensively farmed than it had ever been before.

But it was the homestead and its surroundings that took her breath away. The homestead was just as she had imagined it could be: serene and gracious, carrying the weight of its years with an ease that belied its age. It smelt of the lavender and beeswax polish her grandmother had loved. As Blade carried her suitcase in through the front door she drew in a deep breath, for there, in its proper place, was the portrait of her grandmother.

Tears burned in her eyes. She said huskily, 'I wondered where she had gone to.'

Blade shrugged. 'She belongs there.'

He showed her into her old bedroom, furnished as it had been, although the curtains and paintwork were new. But there, in a silver bowl, was a bunch of Ena Harkness roses, their scent rich and rare and exquisite. Had he remembered how much she loved them?

Eden's mouth trembled for a moment, then firmed.

'Would you like a shower?' he asked, depositing her case on to a small kauri chest. 'Something to eat? No? Then how about changing and coming for a ride with me?'

He was watching her with a little taunting smile, as though he expected her to refuse. Her head lifted. Now was her chance to show him how much she had matured in those endless years away from him. 'I'd like that,' she said calmly.

He saddled up a couple of horses—Thunderer, who recognised her with a polite whiffle of breath, the other a pretty bay mare. As she made friends with her, Eden couldn't help wondering just who Lucky had been bought for. But she said nothing as she mounted her, and nothing as they rode side by side across the green paddocks.

Oh, but it was good to be in the saddle again, good to breathe air with that crisp freshness that existed only in the country! The years in Auckland faded, grew dim; she thought she felt her soul stir and revive, become alive again.

Eden looked around with fascination and a little awe. There was no mistaking the health of the pasture, the sleek, well-cared-for look of Onemahutu, as different as it could be from the run-down property it had been when Blade had bought it. Ahead lay the smooth steepness of Puketotara, serene and grass-covered, all signs of gorse and rush and blackberry and ragwort gone.

'It looks as though everything you touch turns to gold,' she murmured.

'Hardly,' he retorted drily. 'There have been set-backs, but things are going well now.'

At the top of Puketotara she dismounted with him, and walked up to the fenced enclosure beneath the huge totara tree. There were three plaques there now. Sudden tears blurred her vision. After a moment she turned away, stumbling a little.

'Steady,' he said, catching her arm.

Sensation sizzled through Eden's nerves. It had never happened like this, not with any other man. She flinched and tried to pull free, and he said something she was glad she didn't catch under his breath as his fingers closed hurtfully around her arm.

The next moment she was in his arms, held for a long, panicky moment as close to him as his conscience, her slender body imprinted against the warm strength of his. 'Eden?' he said, a quick, blurred sound unlike his usual deliberate speech.

She looked up, saw the mirthless curl of his beautiful mouth, the white line around his lips, the desperate, blazing need in his eyes, and said wretchedly, 'It's no good; it's been three years, and it's still there. I must be out of my mind!'

'Both of us,' he said, and kissed her, kissed her sweetly enough to steal the heart from her body, her mind away.

Three years slid away into oblivion. She had learned a lot in those three years, but this had been what she'd craved for every second of all those long days, this was what she had needed, this was why no other man had had anything more of her than a few kisses.

Blade Hammond was hers, irretrievably, just as she was his. It was as simple, as complicated as that. She had loved him when she was fourteen, she loved him now. In spite of all the betrayals, the lies and the misunderstandings, they had been joined in some unknown fashion since then.

His mouth was demanding, forcing hers open after that first sweet kiss; he made himself master of her responses, plunging her into a sea of sensation, overpowering the tenets she had learned to live by these last years: the caution, the self-discipline, the determined restraint. It all fled, drowned by a primal sensuality, leaving only a need that had grown in the dark through the years to become enormous, all-encompassing.

He lifted her without even drawing a deeper breath, holding her against him while he kissed her eyes and the curve of her cheekbones and the gentle fragility of her temple, the soft wave of hair back from her brow. Eden kept her eyes closed, listening to the rasp of his breath, the hammer of his heart against her.

'Why did you come back?' he asked.

'For the same reason you asked me back. Because I needed to know how I feel about you. How you feel about me.'

He set her down, but he wouldn't let her look away, holding her gaze effortlessly with the electric fire of his. 'How *do* you feel about me?' he asked ruthlessly.

She sighed. 'I'm still in love with you.'

'Still?'

Her mouth trembled, then firmed. 'You knew,' she said without accusation. 'That's why you sent me away, wasn't it? If I hadn't loved you, there would have been no need for me to go.'

He flinched, as though her words were little stones. 'Did I hurt you very much?'

She sighed again. 'I wanted to die.'

'But you survived,' he said softly. 'Better than I did, I think. I love you, Eden.'

Her heart lurched in her breast. She couldn't look away from the need and the hunger, and the openness of his gaze. 'Why did you bring me up here to tell me that?' she asked.

'Because this is where it all started.' He gave a ghost of a laugh, and looked down at the three graves. 'I watched you up here that first day, so gallant, so brave in spite of a situation that would have broken a weaker woman, so proud and erect—and something happened to my heart. It seems appropriate to bring you up here again so that we can close the circle. You are going to marry me, aren't you?'

She nodded, smiling up at him through a glint of tears, and he kissed her, softly, tenderly, and kissed her again. 'Let's go and prepare a marriage, my heart,' he said, whistling to the horses, her hand caught in his as though he would never let it go again.

He made her lie in a lounger out on the veranda while he got her tea, and a slice of magnificent fruit cake cooked by his housekeeper, the wife of one of the shepherds.

'I'm like Gran—I belong here too,' she told him, her eyes resting with pleasure on the velvet lawns and the borders of soft, old-fashioned flowers that she still loved best.

He kissed the hand that lay confidingly in his. 'I know,' he said calmly.

Her eyes filled with unexpected tears. 'Gran left England to be with Grandad,' she said urgently, wanting to reassure him that she was not marrying him for the station, however much she loved it. 'You are where my home is, Blade. More than anything in this world, I love you. If all you had was your two strong hands and your fierce determination, I'd go to the end of the world with you.'

He closed his eyes as though in pain, but when he opened them they were clear and burnished, brilliant sapphires in the golden skin of his face, and his smile was tender.

'I swear that you'll never regret that,' he said quietly, his glance lingering over the fine-boned oval of her face. Leaning over, he kissed her, his mouth gentle yet ardent, as though he was holding himself back.

They were married a month later, a month in which both grew fine-drawn and eager, the flame of passion burning transparently behind the masks of their features. Blade made no attempt to make love to Eden beyond the kisses that they exchanged at every available opportunity, and the sizzling, hungry glances that reassured her.

Desire tormented her, bloomed ripely within her like a rose whose season had come, and if he had come to her she would have given herself with an ardour that subconsciously she knew he needed, but she followed his lead in this, realising that it must be important to him.

Besides, she wished to come to him as virginal as she had left him. For their wedding she wore a dress of soft white organza, youthfully sophisticated, and the pearls Blade had given her the night before. Gardenias wreathed her head, and she carried a bouquet of gardenias and white roses and lilies. They were married in the garden, among friends and a few relatives, one of whom, she discovered with pleasure, was Blade's half-brother—a severe, forbidding man called Kieron Sinclair, with enough of the same golden good looks to publish their relationship.

He arrived in a Rolls-Royce the day before the wedding, and surveyed her with a keenness that would have been intimidating if she hadn't been so blatantly happy. Later in the evening he managed to corner her away from Blade, and said, 'I hope you know what you're getting into.'

She met his glance very coolly. 'Yes.'

He held it for a long moment, then smiled, and she almost gasped at the sudden, smouldering charm. This man was equally dangerous as Blade, in an entirely different way.

'Yes, I think you do,' he agreed. 'Has he told you anything of his childhood?'

'Not a lot.' Her voice was crisp.

'Hmm.' His eyes sought his half-brother's face, rested a moment on the strong, calm countenance, then flicked back to capture hers. His smile had little humour. 'I think you deserve to hear the rest of it, or as much as affected Blade. After the first three years of their marriage, my mother refused to live on our father's station. She'd go up for the holidays, but spent most of the year in Christchurch, close to her parents and her friends. They should never have married; she was—is—the quintessential urbanite. She hated the isolation. We didn't know until I was twelve or so that Blade was our half-brother. By then, of course, we knew him well, and liked him. He's two years younger than me, but we didn't notice the age difference. When Mother finally found out, as you can imagine she was furious. She divorced my father.'

'But he didn't marry Blade's mother?'

Kieron shook his head, watching her keenly.

'I see,' she said. No wonder Blade had wanted a wife who could show his half-family birth and breeding! She made no comment, but Kieron read her emotions in the sparkling glance she shot at him.

His wide, hard mouth tightened. 'Yes, Father was an unregenerate old snob, but I think he did love her, in a way. Anyway, she died about four years after the divorce, and Blade left school and started to work with a cold-blooded determination to earn money. In spite of that formidable self-sufficiency, his childhood has marked him for life.'

'I know,' Eden said sombrely. Blade's mask, the cool, somewhat arrogant watchfulness, the intense strength hidden beneath it, had been forged then.

Kieron smiled, suddenly revealing a potent attraction akin to Blade's. 'However, although he's pretty hard to read, I only have to look at him to realise that the reasons he's marrying you have nothing to do with old anguish and resentment and betrayal.'

She returned his smile, liking him very much for divining her one remaining worry. 'I'm glad you came.'

His wide shoulders moved. 'He's my brother,' he said, 'and I like him, bastard though he can be when he feels like it!'

He was Blade's best man, and Mrs Chalfont had come up to be Eden's matron of honour. Looking around the small group of friends and relatives on the green lawn, Eden felt her heart swell. She would love Blade so much, she vowed, that he would never need reassurance, never wonder whether he came first or second in her life.

They had lunch, drank a glass of champagne with their guests, then changed, she in the bedroom that had always been hers, he in the master suite which from now on she would share. She slid into watermelon linen trousers and shirt, and a pair of slim sandals the same colour.

She was standing admiring the pink diamond he had given her for her engagement-ring, and the plain golden band that meant so much more to her, when he knocked on her door, clad in jeans and a cotton shirt. 'Ready?'

'Yes,' she said, smiling.

They took the Land Rover up on to Puketotara, and there she divided the flowers she had carried into three, putting one small bunch on each of the plaques. For a moment she lingered, Blade's hand warm around hers, then she smiled a little shakily up at him. 'I hope they know,' she said.

His fingers tightened. 'Perhaps they do.'

They had chosen to go to a small cove on one of the tiny harbours north of the Bay of Islands, a journey that ended in a trip in a dinghy propelled by an outboard motor.

Excitement beat high in Eden's throat as she watched Blade stacking the two small suitcases that were all they had brought, except for groceries, into the small craft. There was too much to do on Onemahutu for them to take more than four days, but Blade had promised another holiday during the winter. Somewhere tropical, he'd said, his eyes gleaming azure slivers beneath his dark lashes.

'Think there's going to be enough room?' she asked now.

He grinned. 'I hope so. No, don't try to help; just sit still and I'll pack the stuff in around you.'

The waters danced across the empty little harbour, blue as Blade's eyes, ruffled in places into purple by the passage of tiny gusts of wind. Around them cicadas sang in the trees, blending into the throaty roar of the motor. Five minutes later they were by the small bach that was snuggled down behind a beach where trees came right down to the edge of the gleaming golden sand.

And ten minutes after that they had unpacked the groceries into the fridge and the pantry, their clothes into the wardrobe, and made up the big bed that took up quite a bit of the space in the main room. The bach was perfect for honeymooners, with a small bathroom and laundry combined, a minuscule kitchen off the sitting-room, and three comfortable chairs as well as the bed. Out on the terrace were two loungers and a table.

Eden looked at the bed, but Blade asked casually, 'Is the water warm enough to swim in now?'

So he had remembered! She laughed, and nodded.

'Then why don't you get into your togs, and I'll pull the dinghy further up on to the beach, just in case we get a king tide.'

She came out on to the terrace as he dragged the dinghy up, feeling a little embarrassed in her soft orchid bathing-suit, well aware that she had chosen it for its effect on any male who happened to see her. But her shyness fled as she watched the powerful muscles in Blade's back curl and clench. A faint alarm struggled in her heart. He was so big... would he realise how gentle he was going to have to be?

He looked up, and something leapt from his eyes, impaling her through the heart. This was Blade; he had loved her enough to send her away, he had loved her enough to wait three long years for her to come back. Of course he would treat her with tenderness.

'I'll be with you in a moment,' he said.

The sand burned her feet as she ran across it, but not as fiercely as the need that burned through her body. She shimmered with the heat, feeling it curl in slow increments through her, setting fire to every cell, every nerve.

The water couldn't cool her, nor the soft rhythm of the waves soothe the voluptuous shudders that were working their way down her spine. These last weeks had been so busy that most of the time she had been able to forget her desire, but it had only been leashed, and now she was helpless before it.

She began to swim, back and forth along the beach, her arms slicing cleanly through the water. And then she felt his arms slide around her, and lift her into the air, holding her against the sleek, wet hide of him. Fascinated, her gaze fastened on to the bubbles of air entrapped by the fine, silky dusting of hair across his chest. Her eyes travelled further, lingered on the smooth swell of muscle, the golden-brown pulse that beat rapidly in the strong hollow of his throat, the way the water delineated with gloss and sheen the hard sweep of his jaw, the angles of his face, beloved, softened only for her.

Blade's eyes glittered, blue as the sea. He seemed to be waiting for something. Lifting a wet hand, Eden touched the dark line of his eyebrow, then slid her fingers up into the honey run of his hair, sifting wet amber silk across her fingers, a blind little smile curling her soft mouth.

He closed his eyes for a moment before walking up on to the beach, where he had spread a rug under the swooping branches of a huge old pohutukawa tree.

'I dreamed so many dreams,' he said harshly, sliding her down the length of his body, making no attempt to hide his blatant arousal. 'But this was the one I liked best—to carry you up from the sea and lay you down for me in the shade of a tree, and take you in the open air.'

'I dreamed too,' she revealed, kissing the smooth swell of his shoulder, her mouth lingering, tasting, realising as he drew in a harsh, impeded breath that she had the same effect on him that he did on her.

His hand in her hair tilted her face back; he stared at her as though he still couldn't believe that she had come back to him, and then he kissed her, sliding the straps of her bathing-suit down her arms so that he could kiss the rounded flesh of her breasts, moving with slow, experienced smoothness to reduce her to a mass of shuddering nerves, transforming her to a woman who wanted only this.

He took his time, touching her with those skilful, patient, experienced fingers, encouraging her to touch him until her heart beat so high in her throat that she thought she might die of it, and her body ached with a sweetly fierce need that turned her to liquid.

'Are you ready?' he murmured against the gentle curve of her stomach. His tongue dipped into the hidden circle of her navel, and she flinched at the spear of sensation.

She said in a high wild voice, 'I don't know; I've never felt like this before.'

Blade looked up at that, his eyes sharp points of light, thin rims of blue around the dilated pupil. 'Not even when you——?' He stopped, his expression suddenly blank.

Something intruded into the sensual haze he had woven around her. Eden moved restlessly, wordlessly seeking the heated strength of his body, the weight, the first thrust that would join them forever.

'Not when——?' And suddenly comprehension struck. Eden froze with shock, and he swore, and ran his hand from her throat to the silky curls that hid her from him, saying urgently, 'Hell, I wasn't going to say anything! I'm sorry, darling...'

She lifted her shaking hands to frame his face, silencing him with her mouth. After a moment she pulled away gently, and said against his lips, 'Did you sleep with anyone when I was gone?'

'No.'

She felt the word rather than heard it. 'Neither could I. If it wasn't you, it wasn't going to be anyone.'

His head came down on her breast. 'God,' he said in a shaken voice, 'I love you so much, Eden, that it makes a fool of me! I should have known, but I was always terrified you wouldn't come back to me.'

'You should have known.' Her hand moved through his hair, lovingly. 'Now, are we going to make love, or are we going to talk?'

In answer his face turned, gathered in the aching tip of her breast, and suckled, for a shocking moment just short of pain. Instantly desire flared like brush-fire in Eden's body, and, with a sound that was half-laugh, half-sob, she thrust her hips against him.

He moved like lightning, poised above her, smiling, his handsome features drawn and almost angry.

'I love you!' she cried. 'I love you...'

And then she could speak no longer, because he was within her, slowly, taking his time, but with an inexorable progression that stretched her, made her ready for that last thrust that joined them in a union as fierce as it was long-awaited.

She gasped, and he said urgently, 'Is it hurting?'

'No. I feel—complete.'

His lips drew back from his mouth in a savage smile. 'It gets better,' he told her, and began to move.

It did, so much better that she thought she might die before it was over, so much better that her conscious self slid into dazed oblivion, and she was left with mere sensation—a woman who felt, and loved, and finally cried out in shock and ecstasy as the demands of her body and his sent her into some unknown region where sensation was all that mattered.

Blade followed her into that region almost immediately, his big body shuddering, his hands cruel on her shoulders, and then he collapsed, and Eden lay in the warm, salty air, conscious of nothing but the rhythm of their heartbeats as they slowed into normality.

At last he moved, lying on his back, scooping her so that she lay with her head on his shoulder. If she opened her eyes she could see the glinting blue waters of the bay, empty, secretive, always beautiful. Dreamily she thought that now she understood what happiness was.

'Have you any other dreams?' she asked, laughter threading through the awe still colouring her voice.

She could hear his smile in his voice. 'Such a lot, my heart. Enough to last us a lifetime, I think. What about you?'

She kissed his salt-sleeked skin, then nipped it gently. 'A lifetime might be just about enough time.'

HARLEQUIN PRESENTS®

*A Year*
DOWN UNDER

## WORDFIND #3

```
A D V E N T U R E L M S V B
X G H P O I U B N R B T L Q
A Z P E E H S T D P C A F G
Q E R I K O K N N B K T N R
S X H B S Y O D V E I I J O
N P O F A M Z I O D O O L B
E O L J M B E R Z E P N L Y
D W Z A K L B N X N T Y U N
L O H A T I U V B X D F G H
O Q W R T U I O P L K J H M
G P L C D N A L A E Z W E N
M N B V T O L M V X A S F G
R E O K D N O R T H L A N D
D O N A L D A N Y I P X Q X
```

| | |
|---|---|
| ADVENTURE | MASK |
| BLAKE | NEW ZEALAND |
| DONALD | NORTHLAND |
| EDEN | ROBYN |
| GOLDEN | SHEEP |
| HAMMOND | STATION |

**Look for A YEAR DOWN UNDER Wordfind #4
in April's Harlequin Presents #1546
A DANGEROUS LOVER by Lindsay Armstrong** WF3

In 1993, Harlequin Presents celebrates the land down under. In April, let us take you to Queensland, Australia, in A DANGEROUS LOVER by Lindsay Armstrong, Harlequin Presents #1546.

Verity Wood usually manages her temperamental boss, Brad Morris, with a fair amount of success. At least she *had* until Brad decides to change the rules of their relationship. But Verity's a widow with a small child—the last thing she needs, or wants, is a dangerous lover!

Share the adventure—and the romance— of A Year Down Under!

SOLUTIONS TO
WORDFIND #3

YDU-MA